LICENSED TO KILL. . . .

Harold entered the Funhouse, the Trial
Course which would either claim his life or see
him emerge as a licensed Hunter. The door
clanged shut behind him, locking automatically.
There would be no going back.

Gripping his sledgehammer firmly, Harold
moved on.

Then, from around a bend, came a creature
unlike any he'd ever seen, a Chimaera that
dodged and darted and breathed a blowtorch
blast of fire at him. Harold backed away until,
behind him, a monster scorpion appeared. And
suddenly there was nowhere left to run.
Harold was caught between two mechanical
murderers with only a sledgehammer between
him and death!

VICTIM PRIME

"I had no idea the competition was so
terrifyingly good."

—Douglas Adams

VICTIM PRIME

Robert Sheckley

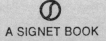

A SIGNET BOOK

NEW AMERICAN LIBRARY

NAL BOOKS ARE AVAILABLE AT QUANTITY DISCOUNTS WHEN USED TO
PROMOTE PRODUCTS OR SERVICES. FOR INFORMATION PLEASE WRITE
TO PREMIUM MARKETING DIVISION, NEW AMERICAN LIBRARY, 1633
BROADWAY, NEW YORK, NEW YORK 10019.

SIGNET TRADEMARK REG. U.S. PAT. OFF. AND FOREIGN COUNTRIES
REGISTERED TRADEMARK—MARCA REGISTRADA
HECHO EN CHICAGO, U.S.A.

SIGNET, SIGNET CLASSIC, MENTOR, ONYX, PLUME, MERIDIAN
and NAL BOOKS are published by NAL PENGUIN INC.,
1633 Broadway, New York, New York 10019

First Printing, June, 1987

1 2 3 4 5 6 7 8 9

PRINTED IN THE UNITED STATES OF AMERICA

Rules of the Hunt •••••

The Hunt is open to anyone eighteen years of age or older, regardless of race, religion, or sex.

Once you join, you're in for all ten Hunts, five as Victim, five as Hunter.

Hunters receive the name, address, and photo of their victim.

Victims are only notified that a Hunter is after them.

All kills must be performed in person, i.e., by the Hunter or Victim himself, no proxies.

There are severe penalties for killing the wrong person.

A Tens winner is awarded almost unlimited civil, financial, political and sexual rights.

Prologue •••••

The Hunt has gone through various stages since its beginning in the early 1990s.

It had its origin in a practice dear to the human heart: the righting of wrongs by violent means.

Back in those early days, everyone wanted to be a Hunter. No one wanted to be a Victim. The peculiar social and psychological rewards of Victim status were discovered only later, in an intermediate period, when the Hunt was set up on the basis of random selection and computerized pairing of Hunters and Victims.

Back then, due to the scarcity of volunteer Victims, the Hunt Organization selected its first victims from those groups that engaged in violence on a regular and habitual basis. These people were, for the most part, death squad participants and terrorists of all political persuasions. They were aggressors who never seemed to get aggressed upon.

Therefore the Hunt Commission thought it appropriate that they should be chosen as Victims, without, however, the later-day formality of advance warning.

This went against the Hunt ethic. But The Organization had to produce "motivated killers" very much against its own aesthetic in order to find people who would proceed with killing.

The Hunters back then were what we would call "motivated" killers. In those days there was very little understanding of the purity of the Hunt, its austere ethic. It would need a later age to perceive in the

Hunt the ultimate art form and to refine the rules so that personal motives could play no part.

Today we can recognize a spiritual quest for what it is. We recognize the dawn of the modern consciousness, the search for the ultimate purity, the conscious acceptance of our place on the great turning wheel of things by consciously going forth to kill or be killed.

Even in those early days, much of our present-day Hunt structure was already in place: the awarding of bonus money, for example, from funds put up by rich liberals, and the use of Spotters to help a Hunter or Victim locate their aggressor. The Hunt Committee tried to maintain some degree of impartiality even in those early days of "righteous killings."

What was apparent, even then, was the Hunt's long-range goal: to convert mankind from its addiction to war by giving it instead the individual two-person death-duel as a panacea for all its woes.

Today, war is as unthinkable as the institution of the Hunt was in the 1990s.

In the Hunt's intermediate stage, during the brief hectic flourishing of Esmeralda, the new rules had just come into being, but they were still flexible. Perhaps some ambiguity was necessary: the Hunt was not yet universal; it was legal only in a single island republic—Esmeralda in the Caribbean, where it was not only the national pastime, but also provided most of the income. This income came from tourists who flocked to the island from all over the world—some to Hunt, others to watch the various contests around them. All took vicarious pleasure in the death of others, and an international audience could watch the infamous Games with their shocking Big Payoff. Watch and enjoy.

Hunters in the earliest days had to contend with a population not yet completely in favor of the Hunt. Although most people found it attractive to one degree or another, the various forces of law and order disapproved and were constantly on the lookout for participants. The police back then tended to treat a Hunter much like any other common criminal.

After many centuries we have rediscovered nature's way of keeping populations in hand. Nature does it the old-fashioned way, by killing people.

So much of the literature in the twentieth and twenty-first centuries had to do with lonely people, growing older and eking out their miserable, solitary existences. That would be unthinkable nowadays. The level of the Hunt has risen to such an extent that old people don't last long: they don't have the speed or agility to scramble away from the gunfire, which fills our streets as rain once did.

Children, conversely, show themselves to be extremely adroit at staying out of the line of fire.

Nobody says any longer, "When will the killing stop?" Now we know that the killing will stop only when life itself stops.

1 • • • • •

At the town meeting in September, the citizens of Keene Valley, New York, voted to arm Harold Erdman with the town's best handgun, a vintage Smith & Wesson .44, and send him south to the island of Esmeralda to enter the Hunt.

Harold had been picked because he had volunteered, had no living kin, was single, healthy, pretty good in a fight, and was considered honest enough to carry out his part of the bargain, namely, to send back fifty percent of his Hunt prize money to the town, assuming he lived long enough to collect any.

In order to get into the Hunt he'd first have to hitchhike and take buses down the American coastline to Miami. From there he could just afford the air fare to Esmeralda, the small island in the southeastern corner of the Bahamas where the Hunt was legal.

The journey from upper New York State to Florida was known to be dangerous in the extreme. There were said to be bandits of incredible ferocity lurking along the way, men fillled with bloodlust and delighting in cruelty. There were devastated regions where foul mists from long-buried industrial dumps burped noxious gases under a traveler's feet, as though the earth were trying to rid itself of its burden of concentrated chemicals and radioactive wastes. A burp like that could poison you in midstride, and you'd be stone dead before you hit the ground. And if you got by all that, there were still the rapacious towns of the south to contend with, places filled with scarcely human creatures who killed anyone they came across, took his belongings, and sometimes ate his flesh.

That's what people said in the word-of-mouth travel advisories by whose means fable is spread, and sometimes fact.

Harold was not much bothered by these stories. He was willing to take a lot of risks to get out of this dying village wedged into a fold of the polluted Adirondacks. He wanted to *do* something with his life, and the Hunt was the only chance open to him.

Harold was large, but he moved lightly for a big man, and he was faster than he looked. He was a big, round-faced, amiable-looking country boy with an ingenuous smile and calculating eyes. He had black untrimmed hair that came down over the collar of his worn red plaid mackinaw, and a few days' stubble on his face. He was twenty-eight years old at the time of his journey and he looked like a bear who's been woken up before he's finished hibernating. Large and sleepy and sort of cute. Which goes to show how much you can judge by appearances.

2 • • • • •

"So you're really going," Allan said. "You're really going to Esmeralda."

Harold nodded. It was an hour after the town meeting.

They had eaten together, and now were sitting on the front porch at Allan's house on Spruce Hill. The sun was just going down over the mountains.

Allan was Harold's best friend. He wanted to go Hunting, too, but he was the only support of his mother and two kid sisters. To leave them in times like these would be the same as killing them. Harold had no one. His mother had died of tuberculosis when he was fifteen. His father, a sour, silent man, had taken off soon after her death, gone to look for work in the south. Nobody had ever heard from him again.

"It's warm all the time down there in the Caribbean," Allan said. "That's what I hear. And they've got everything modern and new. Like in those old magazines in the school. They've got bathrooms with hot and cold running water. They've got restaurants with real food. Everybody's well dressed and happy."

"That's because all they got to do is kill each other," Harold said.

"Well—nothing so tough about that, is there?"

"I don't know," Harold said. "I haven't killed anyone yet. But I figure I can turn my hand to it."

"The trick is not to get killed yourself," Allan said.

"So I hear," Harold said.

"You'll see Nora down there."

Harold nodded. Nora Albright had left Keene Valley two years ago when the buses were still running between Montreal and New York City and stopping at Plattsburgh. She left with four other girls to find work. There was always more work for good-looking women than for men, though some of that work wasn't too savory. The wealthy foreigners, the Asians especially, liked to hire pretty American girls for domestic service, just as Americans once used to hire pretty German and English girls for servants and nannies. The other girls from Keene Valley got jobs in the south, but Nora went all the way to Esmeralda in the Caribbean, the independent little island that lived under the laws of Huntworld. She sent back money regularly.

"You take care of yourself, OK?" Allan said.

"Yes, I'll do that."

"And tell Nora hello from me."

"OK, Allan."

They sat for a while and watched the sun go down over the mountains, the light draining out of the sky, the lonely chill of the north coming down over them. Evening comes down majestically in the Adirondacks. It occurred to Harold that he'd probably never see that sight again. A lot of others, but never that one.

3 ● ● ● ● ●

He left Keene Valley the next day, with the Smith & Wesson, thirty-four cartridges, and two hundred and seventy-six dollars and seventy-three cents they had managed to collect for his expenses. Although it was still September, there was a chill of impending winter in the air—the winter that follows the fall so quickly in upper New York State you'd think they were related.

Everything he had fit into a light knapsack. He carried the Smith & Wesson in his belt, the rounds in his right pants pocket where they'd be handy. He wore his only suit, a heavy almost indestructible serge handed down to him by his Uncle Luke who had died last spring of the T virus.

He took his last look at the mountains, early sunlight glinting off their rocky faces, a scattering of trees still remaining since the last blight, and swung his knapsack into the cab of Joe Billings' truck. He'd said his goodbyes the previous night. They drove off and he didn't look back.

Joe Billings was going as far as Glens Falls to pick up parts for the Farmers' Cooperative tractors. It was getting tougher and tougher to keep the old McCormicks running, and the harvests were so poor they seemed hardly necessary. But there was also a shortage of horses and mules, and the newly introduced yaks hadn't reproduced yet in sufficient numbers to make a difference.

13

Human shortsightedness had finally caught up with America in the late twenty-first century. The forests were gone. The overbred grains and cereals were failing. The American countryside was filled with poisonous places where radioactive wastes or chemicals had been dumped. A lot of the soil had simply given up trying to regenerate itself. Even the air seemed to be going bad. There were no jobs because nobody had any money. Machinery was breaking down and so was the machinery to fix the machinery. Worse, the will to fix things seemed to be gone.

The Cold War still existed and the nations occasionally rattled their sabers at each other. But nobody gave a damn anymore. A lot of people hoped they'd just drop the damned bombs and get it over with. Call this living? Might as well finish it sooner rather than later. Because the good old earth was going to the dogs.

They should never have cut down the forests and jungles. They should have done something about the acid rain when there was still time. Harold was twenty-eight and he could still remember when there was still some green on the brown Adirondack Mountains. The government had gotten serious about ecology about fifty years back. But it was too late and there wasn't enough money. The earth's a big place and bounces back from almost endless amounts of abuse, but people had finally pushed it too far.

There were hardly any animals left in the barren wastes that once had been forested wilderness. The big game animals had gone first, in America and Africa. Then the rest of the earth's delicately balanced ecological system began to come apart at the seams.

The formerly fertile prairies and savannahs dried up and blew away, and it was dustbowl time. Desertification spread, and disasters piled up faster than you could count them. Then the influenza epidemics came, and the other plagues. The survivors scrabbled around a decaying America and tried to get along, to hold on, to wait until things got better. Would things get better? Nobody was counting on it.

Death was everywhere on the face of the North American continent, death by starvation and death by disease and death by the endless varieties of misadventure that man comes up with all by himself.

And still there were more people than the land could support. The human race had exceeded its range, gone beyond the possibility of feeding itself. A universal die-off was inevitable. But that didn't make it any easier to take. Death was so common, so ubiquitous, that it was inevitable that places like Huntworld would come into existence, places where, in paradoxical reaction to the horror of the times, men applauded death, paid men to enact it for them, and rewarded the survivors.

4 • • • • •

After Glens Falls, Harold hitchhiked. A ladies' notions salesman in a New Stanley Steamer gave him a lift. They went past field after field, bare, rocky ribs showing through the dusty soil, the land unproductive ever since the accumulation of past and present chemical and nuclear mistakes had turned Lake Champlain into a cesspool and killed the Hudson once and for all.

Just past sunset the salesman dropped him off at a crossroads south of Chestertown, in a region of stubbled fields and stunted pine. Harold decided to hole up for the night, since hitchhiking after dark was not advisable. It was a mild evening, and he had beef jerky and a canteen of safe water. He found a little hollow sheltered from the wind and out of sight of the road. No use calling attention to yourself.

But somebody must have noticed him anyhow. It was twilight when three men and a dog appeared from over a ridge.

Two of the men were bearded. They were small, skinny men with floppy hats pulled down over their eyes, dressed in shapeless gray and brown clothing. The third man was big and burly, even bigger than Harold, who was no lightweight. He was dressed in worn blue jeans and a faded Civil War–style foragers' cap. He had a weird lopsided grin that made him look dangerous and more than a little crazy.

The dog was some sort of a bird dog, black-and-white-spotted, and it bared its teeth when it saw Harold but didn't growl or make a sound.

"Take it easy, Dilsey," the man with the forage cap said. "She don't mean no harm, mister, and she's right useful for flushing out birds."

"Nice-looking dog," Harold said. He sat with his back against a tree, his knapsack at his feet.

"Stranger to these parts?" forage cap asked.

"Yep. I'm from further north, over to Keene."

"Fixin' to stay around here?"

"Goin' south," Harold said.

"You won't find nothin' down there. Not since that last T virus came through."

"So I heard," Harold said.

Two of the men sat down on the ground, one on either side of Harold and about five feet away. The man with the forage cap sat down on his heels facing Harold. He said, "Maybe you're going to Florida, try your hand at fishing?"

"Might," Harold said.

"Forget it. The fish are all dead and stinkin'. Used to be, you go far enough south you could live off the land. No more, believe you me. You might do just as well staying around here. You could join up with me and the boys. This here is Carl, and his brother Dave. I'm Tag Sanders."

"Pleased to meet you, Mr. Sanders. I'm Harold Erdman. Thank you kindly for your invitation to join you and your friends, but I guess I'll just keep on going south."

"Suit yourself," Tag said. "It's getting late, so if you'd be kind enough as to kick your knapsack over this way and turn out your pockets, we'll take what we need and be on about our business. You can keep your clothes. How's that for fair?"

"Real nice of you," Harold said. "But the truth is, Tag, I don't have much and what I've got I need."

Tag sighed and shook his head. "That's what everybody says. They need what they got! But me and the boys, we need what they got, too."

"You'll have to get it from someone else," Harold said.

"It seems to me," Tag said, "that there are three of us and only one of you, even if you are a big one. I thought I was being pretty nice, offering to leave you with your clothes and your life. Isn't that so, boys? But some people ain't got no manners. Now you got two ways of proceeding. You can hand over that knapsack nice and peaceful-like, and turn out your pockets, or we'll do it for you."

The brothers were edging closer to him. Harold stood up. You could just see the Smith & Wesson in his hand glinting blue in the deepening twilight.

"No," Harold said. "I'll keep what I've got and you keep what you've got. That's the best offer you're going to get. Now get up and get out of here."

Tag and the brothers moved back a few feet. They didn't seem too concerned about the gun. Tag said, "Everybody's got a gun these days, but nobody's got ammo. You got any ammo for that thing, Harold?"

"Don't try to find out," Harold said.

Tag laughed. "Goddam, he's a mean one. The meaner they talk, the less cartridges they got. Dilsey!"

The dog lunged for Harold. Harold fired once, a chest shot which knocked the dog down. Dilsey lay kicking and whining on the ground until Tag knelt down and cut her throat with a clasp knife.

"Poor old Dilsey," Tag said, wiping the knife blade on the grass as he got up. "She was our ammo tester. You're the first pilgrim we come across with ammo and the guts to use it. You got any more shells for that thing, or was that it?"

"I've got all I need," Harold said. "It's getting dark

now, Tag, and I don't want you boys messing with me. I hate to use up cartridges, but you leave me no choice." He raised the gun.

"Hey, hold on!" Tag said.

"Turn around," Harold said in a quiet voice.

"Sure," Tag said, "we'll turn around. You're not about to shoot us in the back, are you? It's OK, boys, we'll just turn around and walk away quiet-like. OK, Harold?"

Tag turned around, then swung around suddenly toward Harold, the knife in his hand held low, coming in for the kill. Harold had been expecting something of the sort. There were bushwhackers in upper New York State—not too many, because the pickings were too thin, but everybody knew they were hard to bluff. Bandits figured that ordinary citizens were reluctant to shoot, even with a gun in their hands, and when they did come across someone who was armed, they counted on a moment's hesitation. As Tag came at him, whooping, Harold shot him in the shoulder, the big old .44 bucking hard in his hand. The brothers yelled as if they'd been hit instead of Tag and took off running. Tag was spun off his feet and knocked down by the impact. He got up quick and ran after the brothers.

Harold let them go. It was getting too dark to shoot, and anyway, he didn't want to kill anyone. Not without getting paid for it, like people said was how they did in Huntworld.

He gathered up his stuff. He stood for a moment over the body of the dog.

"Well, Dilsey," he said, "I'm sorry. But you didn't give me no choice. Now I've got to find another place to sleep, because I sure as hell ain't going to share this hollow with a dead dog." He moved about half a mile away, found another hollow, and camped again. They used to say back in Keene Valley that Harold didn't have a mean streak in his body. But he was determined, very determined, and he didn't push worth a damn.

5 • • • • •

The next day he got a ride into Albany. There he found that he'd have to wait four days for the bus south. He found lodging with the Salvation Army. They had taken over an old warehouse and put a couple hundred men and women in it. They were doing their best to feed everyone, but the soup was getting pretty thin. There was no room inside, but they gave Harold a bowl of soup and told him he was welcome to camp outside.

At last the bus arrived. It was a beat-up old Greyhound with armor plating along its sides. There had been trouble with bandits and hijackers along lonely stretches of the Interstates. The dispatcher said the state police had the situation pretty well in hand, but you could never tell.

The heavy, overburdened old bus made pretty good time down I-95. There was no trouble until they got to Suffern, near the New Jersey state line.

The bus pulled in at the depot outside of town. There didn't seem to be anyone around. Then a little guy in ragged clothing came running out of the depot and hammered at the door. "Open up!" he shouted. "Trouble!"

The driver opened the door for him. "What's the trouble?"

"I am," the guy said, taking a big automatic from his pocket. "Everybody put your hands on your head and stay quiet, nobody gets hurt."

Harold obeyed, like the other passengers. He had

his gun in his belt, but the knapsack was in his lap on top of it and there was no way he could get at it quickly. The guy called out something in a foreign language—Spanish, it turned out to be—and two more guys came into the bus. They were both carrying automatics. One of them had on a big Stetson hat, once gray, now dirt-colored like everything else. His leg was wrapped in bloody bandages, and he could only walk with the help of one of his friends.

He hobbled in, grinned, swept off his hat, and announced, "Good afternoon, ladies and gentlemen. This is a stickup. Please do what my men tell you and nobody gets hurt. Comprende?

He was a skinny little dude and ugly to boot. A face like a monkey only not so hairy. He looked like he had the kind of body that was made for shapeless rags. But he had a nice smile.

"Juan Esteban Lopez, the Catskill Kid, at your service," he said. "I guess you've figured what this is all about. My friends will now go among you and take up a collection. Give generously and give quick, friends, because you don't want to rile us up. You there." He was talking to Harold.

"What is it?" Harold asked, wondering if he should go for his gun anyway.

"Stand up, amigo. Put on your knapsack. You're coming with us. But I'll take the gun." Lopez had spotted Harold's revolver. He took it and put it into one of his own pockets.

"What do you want me for?" Harold asked.

"I'm not going to hurt you," the Catskill Kid said. "I just need some help with this leg."

They finished robbing the bus and went outside, bringing Harold. The Catskill Kid whistled. One more skinny guy came running out of the depot.

"Now, amigo," the Catskill Kid said to Harold,

"just lift me up onto those big strong shoulders of yours and we'll get out of here."

The Catskill Kid gestured with his gun and smiled. Harold lifted him gently to his shoulders. The Catskill Kid let out a hiss of air at the pain of moving that leg.

"Chato," he called out, "get to the car. Start it up. As for you—" He tapped Harold on the shoulder. "Vamos, caballo!"

They ran to the parking lot. The one named Chato, a fat kid of about eighteen, sprinted ahead to a beat-up Buick parked near the depot's exit. When the others got to the car Chato was grinding away with the starter motor, but the engine wouldn't catch.

"No time for jokes," the Catskill Kid said. "What's the matter?"

"I told you about the distributor," Chato said. "I told you it needed new points."

"You said it'd hold out until we got another car."

"I said I *thought* it would hold out."

The starter motor turned more slowly. The battery was about used up. They could hear shouting from the direction of the depot. Men were running out of it. Some of them had rifles.

"We better get out of here," Lopez said. They all scrambled out of the car. On command Harold lifted Lopez back onto his shoulders. They began running toward a low ridge behind the parking lot. Harold could hear firing behind him.

"Goddam," the Catskill Kid said, "Esteban, how come you didn't find those rifles?" Then, to Harold: "Keep your eyes ahead of you, amigo. We don't want to stumble and fall now."

Harold hurried on in a full gallop, up the slope. He ran into a thicket of secondary growth and tore through it, with Lopez ducking down to keep the branches out of his eyes. A thin vine whipped Lopez across the head, and then a branch knocked the automatic out of his hand.

"Hey!" Lopez cried.

"Forget it," Harold said. He kept on going, full speed over the ridge, down into pastureland on the other side, across another road and into woods. He settled down to a steady trot. After another half mile he slowed and came to a stop. He lifted the Catskill Kid off his shoulders and carefully put him on the ground. He took back his own revolver and put it in his belt. He asked, "You got any way of calling those buddies of yours?"

Lopez nodded.

"Better do it. I don't figure those fellows back at the depot are going to follow this far—they'll wait for the state police—but we'd better get together and figure what to do next."

The Catskill Kid cupped his hand around his mouth and made a piercing sound. "Magpie," he said. "Pretty good, huh?"

"Might be, if there were any of them around anymore."

The other three hadn't been far off. They came up, guns out. The Catskill Kid motioned to them to put away their weapons.

He said to Harold, "When I lost the gun, you could have dumped me, gone back to your bus. How come you didn't?"

"Two reasons," Harold said. "First, I got the idea you were a pretty fair fellow even if you are a bandido. I couldn't just leave you there for those passengers. If they caught you they'd string you up."

"And the second reason?"

"When folks get riled up like that," Harold said, "they get hotheaded and hasty and apt to act first and think later. I figured they just might not remember I wasn't one of you. Might even think I was working with you on the inside."

The Catskill Kid looked at him steadily. "Good reasoning. But you do take chances, friend."

"Life's a risky business," Harold agreed.

"You want to come with us?"

"I wouldn't mind," Harold said, "if you're going anywhere in the direction of Florida."

The Catskill Kid laughed. "Of course, south. What's there in the north but starvation? You come along. We gotta get to La Hispanidad, this commune we heard about down near Lake Okeechobee. Plenty of Cubanos there, they take care of my leg. We're going to have to get a car. You up for that?"

"As long as no one gets hurt," Harold said.

"That's up to them," Lopez said. "Me, I don't want to hurt no one. Esteban, give me a gun. Let's get going."

Harold lifted him up to his shoulders. "*Andale, caballo!*" Lopez said. Harold didn't need a Spanish-English dictionary to tell him that that meant giddyap.

6 • • • • •

They crossed the hills to a secondary highway. There was a gas station just outside of a little town called Lakeville, and a boy in a beat-up Ford had just finished gassing up. Before he could pay and drive off, he suddenly found four skinny little guys and one big one standing around him with guns out. The gas station attendant took one look and got inside his station fast and locked the door.

"Hey, boy," the Catskill Kid said, "this your car?"

"No, sir," the boy said. "Belongs to Mr. Billings, who's got the grain store in town."

"Nice sort of guy?" the Kid inquired.

The boy shrugged. "He's OK, I suppose."

"Well, he's going to have to be OK without his vee-hickle. Get out of there, boy, and stand aside."

The boy got out, handed the keys to Lopez, watched as the five men got in. The boy said, "Hey, how about taking me along?"

"You gotta be crazy," Lopez said. "Bandidos don't live long."

"Don't nobody live long. I'd like to come along."

"You'll have to join the next bunch," Lopez said. "Five's about all this car'll take, what with our gear." He turned to Harold. "I could have recruited an army for all the guys asked me could they join. I'd do it, too, if there was anything to take over. Ain't nothing around but more like this. People who still have real money have it too well hid for us to get at. All that's left is the poor hitting on the poor."

They got in and drove off, leaving the boy watching.

"Yippee," Lopez said. "The Catskill Kid rides again. I'm the Hispanic Jesse James, baby. If only I didn't have this shot-up leg. Never mind, we'll get where we going and there'll be a sawbones to patch it up. I hope."

The fat one called Chato did the driving. Lopez had a bunch of roadmaps. He directed them in a southwesterly direction along secondary roads toward Pennsylvania. Harold wanted to know why that way when Florida was due south.

"Simple, baby. You don't want to get anywhere near what they call the Northeast Corridor. We're swinging wide around New York, New Jersey, Baltimore, Washington, Richmond, all that mess. Over that way, state cops and paramilitary patrols stop and check the cars all the time. It's a bad deal. And closer in to the coast, there's a lot of radioactivity from something that happened in New Jersey before I was born. I don't want to get anywhere near that radiation stuff. Not with my delicate cojones."

It took them the better part of two days on back roads to cross Pennsylvania and get down into Virginia. At night they turned into old logging roads and slept near the car. The weather continued mild and they had a fair supply of food. They had to stop at least once a day to gas up, and that was always a dangerous time. It wasn't that the police would be after them for the stolen car, Lopez explained. The cops had more stuff to take care of than a lousy little auto theft.

"So what's the problem?" Harold asked.

"The way it is these days, the cops stop you on routine roadblocks, find you have guns, find you're not local, and that's it."

"What do you mean, that's it? Prison?"

"'They don't want to put people in prison where

they'd have to feed them. You see bodies along the roads every day, and most of them weren't put there by bandidos."

"I've heard stories, but I never really believed the police kill people," Harold said.

"Better believe it, baby, 'cause that's how it is."

Lopez did a lot of talking about La Hispanidad, the place they were going to. "Heard about it back in Union, New Jersey. That's where we're from. This commune in Florida, near Lake Okeechobee. Lot of communes down there, but this one's Cuban. It's run like an Israeli kibbutz—a council, everybody has a vote, everybody does lots of hard work by day and dances at night. Sounds pretty good, huh? That's what I hear. That's for me."

They stayed with the back roads and kept on going through the middle of Virginia and across North Carolina. Then they swung southeast toward the coast. Everything went all right until they reached Leesville, South Carolina, right on the Intracoastal Waterway.

They had gone into a diner in Leesville to get something to eat. It was an ordinary little town, big old trees, some of them still living. They had hamburgers and fries. When they got out to their car there was a police car angled in front of them. A fat cop with a two-day stubble on his jowls was leaning back against the fender of their car, waiting for them.

"You boys mind showing me some ID?"

National ID cards had been in use for some time. They showed theirs. The cop paused for a while over Lopez's card. "OK, boys, turn around, go lean against that car, and spread your legs. I'm going to have to search you." He had his gun out, a Police Positive .38.

"What's the matter?" Lopez asked. "We're just passing through."

"Just do what I tell ya," the cop said. He had a high-pitched good-old-boy voice. "It seems that you boys, or somebody looks a whole lot like you guys, have been pulling some bank jobs north of here."

"We never robbed no bank!" Lopez said with genuine indignation.

"Then you got nothing to worry about. Spread 'em and don't make me ask you again."

"Like hell," Lopez said. He'd had his gun in his pocket with his hand on it. Now he fired through the pocket. The cop staggered back and fell down, a bullet in his thigh.

And then all hell broke loose. Harold couldn't believe how fast armed men were out on the street. Seemed like people in Leesville had nothing to do but sit home with their rifles waiting for trouble. They were shooting and there was no way of getting back to the car.

Harold and the bandidos ducked around a corner and ran. Harold was carrying Lopez on his back and running toward the woods in back of town, and Chato was running beside him. Then Chato said, "Damn!" and blood came out of his mouth and he fell down. Manolo went down next, and then they were in the woods, Harold running full out, and Esteban was to his right, and then Esteban went down and Harold was running alone, pumping with one hand and hanging on to Lopez's legs with the other.

He ran through the woods into swampland. He plodded on through ankle-deep muck and after a while there was no sound of pursuit behind him and he stopped.

He was near a little river or bayou or whatever

they called it, and there was a sort of pier out into the water and a rowboat tied to it and nobody around.

"OK, Lopez," he said, "we are now about to become sailors."

Lopez didn't answer. Harold examined him. The Catskill Kid's eyes were lifeless and staring. As far as Harold could tell he had taken about three slugs in the back, saving Harold's life, though he couldn't be said to have planned it that way.

"Well, damnation," Harold said. He put Lopez down gently. "I'm sorry, buddy," he said to the corpse. "I tried. I'm sorry you won't get to that commune. Somebody else'll have to bury you, Otherwise I sure as hell will never get to see Esmeralda."

He untied the boat, shipped the oars, and started off.

7 • • • • •

Harold rowed all day. The water was green and slimy and overhung with trees and vines, not like the crystal-clear but sterile lakes back home. Harold was new at this rowing game, but he soon picked it up. He had his gun and his knapsack. He wasn't planning on stopping again. If this piece of water went all the way to Florida, he was going to go there with it.

But rowing was slow. He kept up a good stroke, but he figured he was only doing a couple of miles an hour. He'd be all year getting to Florida this way. Still, he thought he'd better stay on the water until he was well away from Leesville.

That night he tied up to a mangrove and slept in the boat. Next day he finished the last of his beef jerky and started rowing again. He rowed most of the day. By nightfall he was hungry and his food was used up. He finished what remained and slept.

The next day he started off again, but soon found himself in a marsh. The going got slower and slower, and there were corpses in the water, lying like half-submerged logs. Harold saw a deserted landing along-side the river or bayou or whatever it was. He rowed toward it. He left the rowboat tied to the dock and started walking.

Just past midday he went through the ruins of a city. Savannah, maybe. It stretched for miles and seemed at first to contain no human life. But Harold soon realized there was someone nearby, dodging

31

along behind a row of gutted buildings, because his passage disturbed the crows and buzzards.

Harold had the .44 handy, but he didn't draw it when the man presented himself, stepping out from between two burned-out buildings. He was a small, portly old man with a white fringe of cloudy hair around his bald skull. He wore a dark, shapeless poacher's coat with many pockets. He looked a little mad, but not dangerous.

"Are you friendly?" the man asked.

"Sure I am," Harold said. "What about you?"

"I am a dangerous fellow," the man said. "But only in the cut and thrust of repartee."

They sat down together near the wreck of the old Dixie Belle Café. The man, whom Harold came to know as the Professor, was a wandering scholar, who gave lectures on a variety of subjects in the towns through which he passed. He was going now to a town just down the line.

"What sort of thing do you lecture about?" Harold asked.

"All sorts of things," the Professor said. "One of my favorite talks is number thirty-two, Why the Human Race Cannot Afford to Stabilize."

"That sounds like fun," Harold said.

"You're an intelligent young man," the Professor said. "I prove in that particular talk that to stabilize is to reach the end of uncertainty. When man reaches the end of uncertainty he will realize that his existence, at least in the terms he imagined it, is futile. Futility, you see, is the enemy of the species, more deadly than the devil himself. It is arguable that the great Indian civilizations of Central and South America perished through the sense of futility brought to them by the Spaniards' invasions. They saw something in the Spaniards, something which on physical terms they could not surpass, could not even get anywhere near. In the terms which the Spaniards had made the real terms, they were defeated. Therefore futile, therefore civilization perished. They thought the Spaniards were godlike—not on a tribal level. They saw their defeat not as a defeat by men but as a defeat by gods."

Harold nodded. "When the gods wipe you out you stay wiped out."

"What defeated them," the Professor said, "was the Weltanschaaung of new technology. The world-transforming activity which a new technology brings, shaping reality."

"You don't happen to have anything to eat, do you, Professor?"

"I was just about to ask you the same thing."

"Then we might as well start walking again."

"To be sure," the Professor said. "And as we stroll I can give you a little sampling of talk sixteen. On Loss of Autonomy."

"Go right ahead," Harold said. "I like to hear you talk, Professor."

"Men distract themselves with love and war and Hunting," the Professor said, "and all manner of joys and cruelties in order to keep from themselves the fact that they are not autonomous, not godlike, but no more and no less than links in the great chain of being which is made up of men, amoebas, gas giants, and everything else. There is evidence aplenty that the ego-centered, individualistic-believing western races are in a decline due ultimately to flaws in their philosophy. They relied too much on intellect. Intellect has been tried and has failed. Intellect may be an evolutionary dead end."

"What should we try next?" Harold asked.

"Nobody knows what's really happening. Or rather, we know what's happening, locally anyhow, but we don't know what it means, if it means anything. We have lost the myth of human perfectibility. Our life span will never be as long again as it was a hundred years ago. Too much strontium in our bones. Too much cesium in our livers. Our internal clocks have been reset to run a shorter time. Our ingenuity finds no way out of this. Our pride is shocked at the intuition of our irreversible racial damage. Our position is that of a patient, dying on the operating table, still trying to plan for the future."

"That's deep," Harold said. "What does it mean?"

"It's not meant to be taken too seriously," the Professor said. "My audiences like a bit of high-flown invective."

"I do like to hear you talk," Harold said. "Some of the things you say set off really weird pictures in my head. I never even knew it was possible for a man to think the sort of things you think. I mean, for me, those things you talk about just don't exist."

"What does exist?" the Professor asked.

Harold thought about it. "Well, just knowing more or less what you have to do and then figuring out ways of doing it."

The Professor nodded. "But isn't there also a presence within you which watches this, comments on it, and ultimately, perhaps, questions it?"

"No, I don't think so," Harold said.

"Perhaps you're a sociopath," the Professor said. "A person unable to feel."

"Hey, that's not right either," Harold said, unruffled. "I feel plenty of things. They're just not the same things you feel."

"Perhaps you are the new man," the Professor said, and his tone made it impossible to decide whether he spoke seriously or in jest.

"Maybe I am," Harold said. "Now let's find something to eat."

"Psychic bilateral cleavage," the Professor said. "Thank God you're basically friendly."

They passed through the ruins of an oil refinery that stretched for miles and miles. It hadn't been used for years. The pipes were rusted out. The concrete of the huge parking-lot-like areas was cracked and crazed. It looked like a graveyard for gigantic machines. Harold found it hard to imagine what they had been used for or why they had needed so many of them.

They came through the refinery area and across the section where highways intersected in complex cloverleaves now overgrown with grass and even with some small trees. There were small, brightly colored flowers along the curving parallel lines of Route 95. The flowered roadways with their precise curves looked as though a giant had laid out a garden.

Beyond this they came to low green hills. They crossed these and came out the other side, into fields with a path between them, leading to a collection of low buildings.

"That is Maplewood," the Professor said.

There was one larger building in the center, low and long and capable of holding hundreds of people, perhaps thousands. Harold had never seen one before.

"That is a shopping mall," the Professor said. "At one time it was the central artifact of American life. It was to the Americans what the atrium was to the Romans or the plaza to the Spaniards, the great place of assemblage where one comes and ritually buys foods and tries to arrange romantic assignations with attractive members of the preferred sex, whichever that might be."

"Professor," Harold said, "you got a real strange way of looking at things. Let's go down there and talk with those people and see if we can get some food."

8 • • • • •

In the town the drums were sounding to signal the arrival of strangers. Many of the isolated little towns of America made use of drums, because the Indians had used drums and the new tribalism called for white, colored, and Hispanic men to act tribally. To act tribally meant to use drums. The drumming wasn't very good because this was a largely white town and the inhabitants, many of them, didn't have much of a sense of rhythm. But they were earnest about it. The spirit was there.

"Ahh, you come just in time for the big potakawa," a spokesman said, coming out of the crowd to greet them.

"That's great," Harold said, "but what's a potakawa?"

"Potakawa," the spokesman said, "is an old Indian word for Red Tag Day. That is the day on which, in accordance with the ancient traditions of our tribe, everything goes on sale at half price."

"I see that we have indeed come at an auspicious time," Harold said.

"Foreign buyers are always welcome," the spokesman said. "You honor our village."

"They seem like real nice people," Harold said later as he and the Professor were resting in a well-appointed room in the town's guest house. They had eaten well—a tasty stew of opossum and eel with okra, a specialty in the region.

The town was called Maplewood and the guest house was called Maplewood Guest House. And the room they were in was the Maplewood Room. "But the wood's pine," Harold noted, tapping it with his knuckles.

"Doesn't matter," the Professor said. "Maplewood does not refer to a type of wood—that is to say wood of maple—but is instead the name of an entirely different entity, namely this town."

"Well, I guess I got a lot to learn about," Harold said. "What do we do now?"

"I believe," the Professor said, "that we are supposed to buy something."

"Nothing hard about that," Harold said.

"The problem is," the Professor said, "one has to buy the *right* something. Otherwise they get offended."

"How offended? Enough to kill?"

The Professor shrugged. "Why not? Dying's no big deal. And who cares what happens to a stranger?"

"Well," Harold said, "let's go out there and buy the right thing. Do you have any idea what that might be?"

"They change it every year," the Professor said gloomily.

Just then the spokesman popped his head in the door. "Time to buy something," he said, smiling brightly.

Harold and the Professor rose and followed the spokesman out to the brightly decorated supermarket. The chief was in full tribal costume, which consisted of a paisley Chardin jacket, trousers by Homophilia of Hollywood, and shoes by the fabled Thom McAnn. These were the clothes which businessmen had once worn as they went about their mysterious errands of power in the great cities, back when there had been great cities.

Harold and the Professor followed the spokesman outside to the supermarket. The shelves were all bare. Harold was surprised at this at first until the Professor reminded him that he was taking part in a ritual, that is to say, something that is not the thing itself. The real merchandise was kept outside, and where the choice of life or death would have to be made.

Outside the supermarket there were long rows of booths like an oriental bazaar. These booths were constructed of simulated deerskin as in the ancient Indian fashion, and were suspended upon tall ribs of iron painted to simulate wood. In front of each booth the owner sat cross-legged, with his wife or a son or daughter nearby to help wait upon the customer; for in the ancient Indian tradition the customer was sacred.

The goods that Harold saw, piled on little tables in front of the booths, were not the sort of goods he'd seen in Mr. Smith's general store back in Keene Valley. Mr. Smith, for example, had not stocked broken light bulbs; but here was an entire window display of them. Here was a shop selling nothing but broken furniture, another shop with smashed china. Here was one that had scraps of painted canvas. There was a booth of farm machinery, hopelessly wrecked.

Harold realized that nothing in this supermarket was whole and usable—it was all what the Professor called "symbolic." Yet he was supposed to pick something. But what?

His forehead creased. Why not let the Professor do the picking? He was an educated man who was supposed to know about such things.

He looked at the Professor and saw the look on his face. It was a look that said, "You do it."

Harold knew that look. It was the slave look. It was the look that said, "I'm too scared to choose so you'd better do it for both of us."

Harold turned quite abruptly, reached into a booth, and plucked from it a crowbar about three feet in length and slightly bent. "How much for this?" he asked the spokesman.

The merchant conversed with the spokesman in language Harold did not understand. This town spoke its own patois as well as the generally accepted Spanish and English.

The shopkeeper, his face a grotesque mask portraying willingness to serve, said, "Since it's Red Tag Day and since I like your face we'll make it two dollars."

The crowd pressed forward as Harold took his worn billfold out of the back pocket of his shiny-assed blue jeans. He opened it slowly, and the people gaped and pressed closer. You'd think they'd never seen something like that before—somebody buying something. It was religious with them, of course, that would have to account for it. The Professor held his breath as Harold handed over his two dollars.

"Now," the spokesman said, "you must answer the question."

"All right," Harold said. His face was peaceful, untroubled.

"Why did you buy the crowbar?"

Harold smiled. He stood tall, head and shoulders above any of them. The crowbar in his fist came back behind his shoulder, and the crowd fell back.

"I bought it," Harold said, "to crack me a few skulls if anyone started messing with me."

There was a moment of silence as the crowd digested this. "And also," Harold said, "it's the custom where I come from to pick something useful."

It took a second for it to sink in, and then a vast sigh went through the crowd. It was like the sound of a giant amen. Harold had said magic words which made him, temporarily at least, a brother like the rest of them. Harold had told them he came from a place that had customs, just like Maplewood had.

9 • • • • •

In a few hours he had reached the coastal highway and started hitchhiking again. Two days later he crossed the border into Florida.

He made pretty good time down Florida, considering the state of the roads. Truckers stopped for him because he was big enough to lend a hand if something had to be loaded or unloaded down the line and because he didn't look mean. The quick impression was that Harold looked pretty much OK. He picked up his last ride outside of the disused Cape Canaveral base. The driver was carrying a load of timber and iron punchings and was hoping to sell them or trade them for food. That ride took him the rest of the way down to Miami.

Miami looked even worse than Harold had expected. The big buildings along Flagler Boulevard were fire-streaked concrete shells, burned out, gutted, and stripped. The people on the streets were furtive, dark, dressed in rags. The T virus had really hit hard here. There were bodies on the streets. Even the palmetto palms looked scrubby and tired and ready to give up. It was depressing to see that it was as bad in the south as in the north. But there was nothing he could do about it. He was going to Esmeralda, where a man could make a living.

Esmeralda was a couple hundred miles away across the Caribbean, in the southeastern corner of the Bahamas near Cuba and Haiti. Harold asked around and was sent to the Dinner Key docks. He had hoped to work his way across, island to island. But the dark-skinned fishing-boat crews didn't seem to speak any English, and they shook their heads when he tried them in broken Spanish. After three days of this, sleeping on the beach with his gun in his hand in case of trouble, he decided to spend some of the money he had been hoarding ever since leaving Keene Valley and take the plane, the Flying Cattle Car, over to Esmeralda.

10 • • • • •

The flight was full. Harold sat across the aisle from three middle-aged men who were teasing one of their group, "good old Ed," about his supposed intention of getting into the Hunt once they reached Esmeralda, an idea which Ed denied. Ed was gaunt, dressed in a Montgomery Ward glen-plaid suit. He had homely, wind-reddened country features and a shock of iron-gray hair. He was a little older than his friends. He was trying to laugh off their witticisms and was getting flustered.

Harold got bored listening to them after a while and went to the scruffy little cabin lounge. He had spent very little money since leaving Keene, so now he treated himself to a beer. He was halfway through it when good old Ed came back to the lounge, glanced at him, and sat down nearby. Ed ordered a beer, took a sip, chewed at his heavy lower lip for a while, then said to Erdman, "I hope we weren't making too much noise back there."

Harold shrugged. "It didn't bother me none."

"They like to kid me a lot," Ed said, "but they don't mean no harm by it. We've known each other since we was kids. We all still live within twenty-five miles of where we grew up in Cedar Rapids, Iowa. That's something, eh? They rag me like this because my hobby is guns. I've competed in a couple of fast-draw competitions in the midwest. Trying to outdraw a machine, of course, not a real opponent. But I figure you need a lot more than a fast draw if you want to compete in Huntworld. It's not for me. I'm just going to see the sights."

There were other people in the lounge, and they began getting into the conversation. An old man with a face like a crumpled brown paper bag told them that the Huntworld they were going to was a pale imitation of what Hunting used to be like back in the good old days when it was legal in the United States.

"Back then the Hunts computer was like God. Impartial. Fair to all. The rules were simple and strict and straightforward. Not like nowadays, when you hear strange stories about Treachery Cards and Vendetta Cards and similar tomfoolery. It's commercialism at its worst, and the government of Esmeralda encourages it. I've even heard that some of those gunfights are fixed."

Another man, tall, with a rectangular, tanned, even-featured face shadowed under a white Stetson, looked up from his beer and said, "I doubt that, about the Hunts being fixed. It's hard to fix a gun battle when both parties are armed."

"People are up to anything these days. I'm Ed McGraw, by the way. From Iowa."

"Tex Draza, from Waco, Texas."

The three men talked for a while, then Harold finished his beer and went back to his seat. His seatmate, a beefy man with a sunburned face and wearing a Hawaiian shirt, had been asleep since Miami. Now he awoke abruptly.

"Are we there yet?"

Just then a tired-looking steward in a soiled green jumpsuit made an announcement over the crackly public-address system. "Ladies and gentlemen, if you'll look out the right side of the plane, the island of Esmeralda is now in view."

Through the scratched Plexiglas Harold could see

an island, dark against the bright mirror of the sea, growing in size as they approached. Its hills were clad in pine and scrub oak, and its black sand beaches were frothed by a thin line of breakers. Far in the distance Harold thought he could make out the hazy coastline of another, bigger island. "What's that over there?" he asked his seatmate. The beefy man squinted and shrugged. "Hell, that's Haiti."

The jet descended rapidly over Esmeralda and began the turn that would take it to Morgantown Airport on the side of the island fronting the Mouchoir Passage.

The seat-belt and no-smoking signs came on and the stewardess announced, "Ladies and gentlemen, we will be landing in Esmeralda in a few moments. Please extinguish all cigarettes. Thank you. And enjoy your stay in Huntworld."

11 • • • • •

It was a pleasant and efficient airport, bright and shiny, in stark contrast to Miami's. Palm trees in pots, low ceilings with fluorescent panels, pastel colors. Vaguely Caribbean murals on the walls. Customs and immigration were swift but thorough. They didn't seem to care much about who came in. Harold's suit, dirty and sweat-stained, didn't even rate a glance from the neatly uniformed policeman who waved him through with the rest of the passengers. And there he was, just like that, in Esmeralda, home of Huntworld.

He made his way through the crowded airport to the taxi and bus loading areas outside. There were about a hundred people waiting for transportation. Harold shouldered his knapsack and walked away from the crowd, hoping to find a ride into the city but planning to walk if necessary. He had gotten halfway around the building when a low white open sports car stopped beside him.

The driver said, "If you're going into Esmeralda, you're walking in the wrong direction."

"Well, hell," Harold said. "How about giving me a lift?"

The driver swung the door open. He was a big, tanned man, almost as big as Harold but a lot better-looking. His face was classically Italian: olive-skinned, with melting brown eyes and a dark stubble on his well-shaven chin. He wore a camel's-hair cashmere sports coat and a pale blue paisley ascot.

"Come here to Hunt?" he asked.

"I'm considering it," Harold said.

"Permit me to introduce myself," the driver said. "I am Mike Albani. Everybody knows me. I am a first-class Spotter."

"A Spotter? What's that?"

"I thought everybody knew about Spotters," Albani said. "We're what you might call the Hunter's advance men. We provide whatever you need: cars, weapons, ammo, and above all, information. We set up your kill for you, or figure out who's after you when it's your turn to be Hunted."

"What do you get for that?" Harold said.

"All it costs you is one quarter of your Huntworld advance plus expenses. Believe me, it's worth it. What are you going to do, buy a telephone book and a roadmap and try to Spot for yourself? Who's going to set up your safeguards, figure out the enemy's defenses? That's my job; I'm good at it. So if you do decide to Hunt I'd like to recommend my services. I can be hired by the hour, day, or duration of the Hunt."

"Thanks for telling me that," Harold said. "I'll keep it in mind."

"Maybe you'd like to see our famous sights? I also arrange scenic and nightlife tours."

"Do I look like I'm ready for a nightclub?" Harold asked.

Albani had taken in Harold's cheap heavy smelly serge suit and clumsy workboots still caked with red Georgia mud. "I thought you might be an eccentric. Sometimes they're very wealthy."

"If I was a rich eccentric," Harold said, "I'd dress just like you."

"Maybe you'll strike it rich, who knows? Hunting pays well. Where can I drop you?"

"I don't know," Harold said. He had thought he'd

go straight to Nora's address, but now he decided against it. He had about a week's whiskers on his face and his body was damned near as grimy as his clothes. "Where can I get a cheap hotel?"

"The Estrella del Sur, right in the heart of downtown. Costs just a little more than some of the South Dockside places, but at least they don't rob your room. Not while you're awake, anyhow."

"Thanks, that's good to know," Harold said.

They were on a four-lane highway crossing a flat plain. There were souvenir shops and flat-roofed factories along the road. Billboards advertised hotels, restaurants, suntan oil, cigarettes. Palm trees here and there reminded you that you were in the Caribbean. It was the biggest show of prosperity Harold had ever seen, outside of television programs that showed you how things used to be in America before the bottom dropped out of everything and Mother Nature pulled the plug. Soon they were in the city of Esmeralda itself. Harold was amazed by the cleanliness of the streets and the lack of beggars.

"People look pretty prosperous here," Harold said.

"We get tourists year-round. Esmeralda is very popular among Europeans, and even Asians are starting to come now. It keeps the economy going."

"You get that many people coming here to Hunt?"

"Oh, most of them say they're just here to watch." Albani smiled maliciously. "They're not planning to kill anyone. Oh, no, they just want to visit this quaint island where men wear weapons and duel and Hunt each other. They want to watch safely behind the bulletproof windows of our cafés and restaurants. So they say. But it's interesting how many of them end up joining the Hunt. Something in the air, I suppose. Good thing for us, too, all those people coming here to kill each other off. The island would be depopulated in a year if the Hunters weren't regularly replenished from the outside. We don't have much of a birthrate, you know. People don't come here to raise families."

Albani pulled to the curb in front of a four-story building that had seen better days. A faded sign on its front said it was the Estrella del Sur.

"Have a nice stay," Albani said. "And if you decide to Hunt, anyone can tell you where to find me. I'm the best and I work cheap."

12 • • • • •

Esmeralda was a long low island near Great Inagua in the southeastern corner of the Bahamas, almost within sight of Haiti. In 2021 a bankrupt Bahamian government had sold the island, sovereignty and all, to a group of international investors with headquarters in Berne, Switzerland. It seemed a reasonable move to the Bahamian government of General Lazaro Rufo, whose government, recently established by coup d'etat, was desperately in need of hard currency. What did one island matter, especially a barren one like Esmeralda, when you had seven hundred others to worry about? The price was right and the island was worthless.

It was worth plenty to the Huntworld Corporation, an international consortium of wealthy men dedicated to the sound principles of profit and quick turnover. Murder was the ideal product, even better than drugs, since the users supplied everything—their lives, their guns, and their deaths. Murder, when done in an orderly and businesslike manner and only with consenting parties, was even socially acceptable. And it had obviously great potentiality as a sport for people who had tried everything else.

Although many governments had expressed an interest in letting Huntworld operate on their territory, the corporate heads of the Huntworld Corporation decided to put it on a country of their own. They would avoid problems with government by the simple expedient of being government. And as a further inducement to investors, they would collect taxes instead of paying them.

From its inception, the Huntworld project was imaginatively conceived and well funded. The island's shabby little capital of Morgantown was torn down. An architectural master plan for a complete new city was drawn up and carried out in record time. The new city of Esmeralda was not the usual steel-and-glass rabbit warren that the modern world had developed in its long struggle to free itself from any hint of good taste. The plan for the city of Esmeralda was frankly medieval and didn't even have a space allocation for a shopping mall. About half of its buildings were made from a light-colored rock mined from calcareous deposits on the island. But major structures on the island like the Hunt Academy and the Coliseum were built of imported limestone and Italian marble. From its very beginning Esmeralda looked like a graceful old colonial city, vaguely European in appearance, a Renaissance city springing up like a *fata morgana* on the low coral surface of Esmeralda.

The tranquil tropical island with its beautifully sculptured and well-antiqued city was a prime tourist attraction all by itself, even without the added incentive of legalized murder. You could come to Esmeralda and enjoy the glamour of the past, but with all the convenience of the fun-loving present.

Not only did Huntworld provide fun and danger in a setting of great natural beauty, it was also a place for the contemplative scholar. It had a world-famous museum of Assyrian and Hittite antiquities, purchased entire from a bankrupt England and shipped to Esmeralda to add a little class to the operation. It had a well-funded Oceanographic Institute that rivaled Monaco's. And there were the famous resorts, the Rockefeller Hilton, the Holiday

Ford, the Dorada del Sur, the Castillo, the Cantinflas; and the golf courses, the tennis courts, the unrivaled underwater fishing, the cuisine from five continents.

And if you didn't happen to have the price of a first-class vacation in your electronic bank account, Huntworld had a cut-rate nonstop carnival village at DeLancy's Beach on the southern tip of the island. This was where the renowned Saturnalia began each year, Esmeralda's own unique version of Carnival or Mardi Gras.

The final ingredient in the mix was the Hunt, that peculiar institution in which men risked their lives against each other in accordance with a minimum of rules. The Hunt was a sort of controlled lawlessness, a celebration of the darker emotions. What you could do legally in Huntworld was precisely what the world had been trying to get rid of since the beginning of recorded time. Without success.

Although a lot of the world was in bad shape, Huntworld was doing just fine. People came from all over to witness the debasement of its morals and the miracle of its favorable balance of payments. Murder was always good business. Huntworld also dealt in sex and drugs, thus completing its investment in the things men treasure.

In the rest of the world, men distrusted change and shied away from novelty. Fashion had disappeared. The arts had become almost exclusively interpretive rather than innovative. People tended to look alike and act alike. Conformism was in. The sciences had suffered a decline. Medical science had changed since its Faustian days in the twentieth century. Doctors no longer tried to preserve individual lives indefinitely. Now the goal was to keep as much of the dwindling, disease-ridden population going as possible.

In theoretical physics, there hadn't been an important new cosmological theory in over a hundred years, and no new subatomic particles had been found in the last thirty. Science was stagnating for lack of funds, and there was no objection to that in the world at large. People thought it was nice to have science slow down for a while. Everyone knew that science was dangerous. It was science, after all, which had brought the atom bomb and all the other troubles out of its Pandora's box of bright ideas. Maybe it was time to put a moratorium on bright ideas, time to stop trying to improve things, or even learn things. It was time to keep your head down.

The current quietistic period in world affairs came about as a result of the nuclear war between Brazil and South Africa in 2019. Who could have predicted that a dispute over fishing rights in the South Atlantic would result in a war that would directly or indirectly kill some twelve million people on two continents and very nearly pull the entire world into self-destruction? The present era of stagnation dates from the conclusion of hostilities between the South American Federation, that gaudy but short-lived brainchild of the ideologue Carlos Esteban de Saenz, and Greater South Africa under the black ruler Charles Graatz.

The Fish War, as it has been called, came to an end on June 2, 2021, with the sudden and still-unexplained death of Saenz. The dictator's death, hours after the end of the second nuclear exchange between the two nations, put the South American ruling council into disarray. The long-planned interdiction of the Zambesi basin had to be postponed, awaiting the emergence of a new chief of state. This presented an unequaled opportunity for the South Africans.

But the unexpected occurred. With his enemies' forces temporarily out of combat, with a chance to press his advantage home, Charles Graatz of South Africa confounded everyone. Instead of taking advantage of the situation, he unilaterally suspended hostilities and disclaimed any further interest in the disputed fishing rights.

He was quoted as saying, "Trying to find an advantage in a situation like this is madness. Why kill the world over a mess of fish? If no country can step back from the brink except when decisively defeated, war will be perpetual and everlasting. Speaking for my Zulu constituency, and for our white, black, colored, and oriental minorities, I say, if it means so much to them, let the South Americans have the fish."

The South Americans, under newly elected General Retorio Torres, were not to be outdone on a point of pride. Torres declared that the fishing dispute had been a matter of principle rather than of fish, but that pride was a still greater principle than Principle itself. Not to be outdone in reasonableness, he suggested that they let the UN handle this one.

The crisis ended so quickly and unexpectedly that the world was caught in the curious position of having no other immediate crisis upon which to go to war. Nor was any country quick to fill the crisis gap, as it came to be called. Against all expectation, there was peace.

People were tired of the long tension of living on the brink of annihilation. The excruciating questions of nationality, race, religion, politics, social theory, and political power seemed unimportant in the face of the new universal imperative: Don't Rock the Boat.

Finding itself, accidentally, as it were, in a state of

peace unprecedented since the beginning of civilization, the world at large decided that it was a good time to let everything stay just the way it was, a good time to stop pushing the dear old national interest and let some of the radioactive waste laid down by the impatient twentieth century get rid of some of its leaking half-life without adding more to it.

It was time to let up on the atmosphere, time to give the planet and everyone on it a chance to breathe.

Time to hold fast, rest easy, just stay in your places.

Out of this arose the period of peace called, variously, the Truce of Exhaustion, the Time of the Great Stagnation, and the Beginning of the New Dark Ages.

One odd statistic showed up. It seemed that men of prime age, the young men who were no longer being killed in the flower of their youth in one senseless war or another, were, many of them, seeking other ways of getting killed.

It was almost as if a part of the population found it necessary to kill itself off periodically, if not for one reason, then for another, or for no reason at all.

It was irrational but inescapable. How else to explain the great prosperity of a place like Huntworld?

13 • • • • •

Just as he was about to enter the hotel, Harold heard people shouting, heard the quick slap of running footsteps. He looked around and saw a man running down the sidewalk toward him. Twenty feet behind, another man was chasing him. The second man had a gun.

As the first man rushed past Harold, the second man fired. Harold, pressed back hard against the wall of the hotel, heard something fly past his right ear and chunk hard against the granite. A bullet had missed him by less than an inch. He looked at the chipped place on the wall. Pursuer and pursued hurried past, into a side street.

Harold went into the hotel and up to the desk. The manager, dark-skinned and white-haired, wearing soiled white slacks and a T-shirt, looked up from his newspaper. "Five dollars a night in advance," he said. "There's a bath in the hall."

"I almost got killed out there," Harold said.

"Can't be too careful around here," the manager said. "The traffic is atrocious."

"No, it was a bullet."

"Ah, Hunters," the manager said, waving his hand in a gesture that might have meant "Boys will be boys." "You want a room? Sign in here."

The room was small, white-curtained, reasonably clean, with a single bed and washbasin. There was a french window with a view of a cobblestoned plaza with a statue in the middle of it.

Harold took his knapsack and went down the hall to the bathroom. He bathed and scrubbed himself clean, shaved, then washed his suit and changed into jeans and a blue workshirt. He went back to his room, found hangers, hung up his stuff to dry.

There was a telephone in the room. Harold took the slip of paper with Nora's telephone number out of his worn wallet. He had to go through the hotel switchboard, and it seemed to take forever, but at last the call went through.

"Nora? Is that you?"

"Who is this?"

"Guess."

"I don't want to play any games. Is this Frank?"

"Goddam, Nora, you mean to tell me you really don't know who this is?"

"Harold? Is that really you? You're here in Huntworld?"

"I guess I am," Harold said.

"But how did you ... never mind, we can talk about it later. Want to come to my place for a drink?"

"Does a pig like to wallow?"

"You come on over." She gave him directions.

Out in the streets the crowds were dense and the air was filled with the smell of frying spiced oil, roasting meat, sweet-sour wine, and faintly, persistently, cordite. The people he passed were unbelievable. They were wearing, among other things, furs, bathing suits, Greek tunics, Roman togas, Renaissance headdress, American Indian loincloths, and Turcoman robes. There were other costumes Harold could not identify. This was a pretty funny place, just like people said. But it was a prosperous place, and Harold liked looking at that. He had never seen such a clean shiny place before. There were trees planted along the sidewalks, and it was nice looking at trees again. He'd heard there was a whole forest on the island, and he wanted to see it.

He had to ask directions a couple of times, but at last he arrived at the small plaza with the fountain which Nora had described to him. He found the entrance to her building, marked by a stone arch. He went through, up two flights of stone stairs, and then it was the first door on the left. He rang the bell.

The door opened, and there was Nora. "Well, come on in," she said.

14 • • • • •

Nora was pretty much the same as two years ago when he'd seen her last, small and well-shaped with cute little features and smooth short blond hair like the girls in those hair ads. Her apartment was small but it was nice. She poured a beer for him.

"Harold, however did you get here? You had that good job at the synthetic-meat plant. I never thought you'd leave that."

Harold had been the best marbleizer old Claymore had ever seen. It was a job that had to be done by hand, because all the machinery in the plant was worn out and breaking down and the automatic marbleizer never had worked right. And there was no way to get it fixed, because there was no machine shop closer than Albany. Harold used to stand in front of the assembly line all day and hand-marbleize the gelatin blocks, six inches by three by three, as they came by him on their flyspecked trays. Each block weighed exactly one kilo, and they were all rose-colored. After Harold got through with them they went on to the texturizers.

"Well, I didn't exactly leave that job," Harold said. "It left me. There I was, top marbleizer in the factory, and what does old Claymore do but decide to quit marbleizing his synthetic steaks and see if anyone objected. It costs money to marbleize those gelatin meat blocks with real fat. Gives them some taste, though. So anyhow I got laid off. You know there's no other work around Keene Valley."

Nora nodded. "I know it only too well. Before I left I was clerking twelve hours a day at Simmons's in Lake Placid and barely making enough to keep alive on."

"Fred Simmons is dead," Harold said. "Fell into one of the old quarries somehow. His sister runs the store now."

"I don't wish anyone dead," Nora said, "but he was one mean man. Harold, how did you happen to come here?"

"The town fathers asked me to come down here and check up on you."

"Be serious!"

"They need more money from outside," Harold said. "They need help to keep going through the winter. I volunteered to come down here and see if I could make some money."

"Hunting?"

"Unless bank robbing is easier."

"You can forget about that. Murder may be legal here, but robbing a bank is considerd a crime somewhat worse than treason."

"I was only kidding," Harold said. "About robbing banks, I mean. I forgot to tell you that Sam Kanzile that used to go with the Berger girl got caught by one of those packs of wild dogs and pretty well tore apart."

"Always nice to hear the hometown gossip," Nora said. "What do you do back there for fun nowadays?"

"The nightlife is about the same as when you were there. Drinking coffee at Mrs. Simpson's diner. Sometimes when I'm in a real reckless mood I climb up that old slag heap outside of town that the mine people left us. It seems a fit place for a man to sit, on top of a mountain of crap he and his neighbors built with their own hands."

"They say that slag's radioactive."

"Hell, so's the whole damned town. They say it's bound to get you if something don't beat it to it first."

"You really are a whole lot of fun," Nora said. "That's why I left Keene Valley. There never was any fun and people always talked depressing."

"Is death a depressing subject?" Harold asked. "Funny, I thought that was what Huntworld was all about."

"It is," Nora said. "But death here is sorta nice, while death back home is just a plain drag. Want another beer?"

"You know it, sweet lady."

She laughed and went off to the kitchen. Harold got up and walked around the room. There were framed photographs on one wall. There were pictures of Nora's parents. There was a picture of Ausable Chasm and another photo of Lake Placid. There was a framed photo of somebody he didn't know, a big rugged-looking man, middle-aged, balding, tan, smiling confidently into the camera

"Who's this?" he asked when she came back.

"That's Johnson," Nora said.

"Oh, of course," Harold said. "Johnson. I guess I should have known that. Nora, who in the hell is Johnson?"

Nora laughed. "He's this guy I was living with. I met Johnson over in Miami and I came here with him. This is his apartment. Was, I mean."

"What line of work was he in?"

"He was a Hunter. Pretty good Hunter. His last kill was sort of funny. He was a Victim that time, and the guy hunting him turned out to be an Indian. From India, I mean, not America. Can you beat that? They're supposed to be so ultra-nonviolent, aren't they? Little fat brown guy with a turban. A turban! Can you believe it? Johnson said if he'd known the guy was going to wear a turban he could have saved himself the cost of a Spotter."

"Nice sense of humor, Johnson," Harold said.

"He could be real funny. There are his trophies."

Harold walked over to the wall she indicated. There were four bronze plaques mounted on varnished mahogany. Each one was an official acknowledgment of a kill.

"Where's the famous Johnson now?" Harold asked.

"Boot Hill, just outside of town. Some guy with glasses from Portland, Oregon, got him. You can never tell, can you?"

"No, you never can. Listen, Nora, have you got anything to eat around here? I've got money, I can pay you for it."

"I'll do better than that," Nora said. "I know a real nice place to eat where the manager owes me a favor."

"Now how did that happen to come about?" Harold asked.

"Don't ask silly questions, you big jerk. Everyone's got to make a living as best they can. The food's good." Suddenly she ran over and hugged him. "Oh, Harold, it's really good to see you."

15 • • • • •

The restaurant was at the end of a twisty cobblestoned street and then down an alley, and then down three steps into a cellar. Inside the place had yodeling waiters in lederhosen and a three-piece gypsy band. It had a tiny circular dancing floor illuminated by shocking-pink baby spots. The atmosphere was thick with ambiance and cigar smoke and liberally laced with animated conversation in five different languages. The manager winked at Nora and gave them a table near the dance floor and sent over complimentary drinks.

Harold was too hungry to talk much until he had wolfed down the first course, a marinated fish thing called seviche, damned good, too. He was able to slow down over the next course, a steak made of real meat, and get some information.

"Listen, Nora, how much do they pay you to get into this Hunt?"

"Two thousand dollars signing-up money once you qualify, either as Hunter or Victim. Three thousand more when you make your kill. That's for your first."

"And after that?"

"It goes up after that for each kill."

"Do you get to choose whether you'll be a Hunter or a Victim?"

"No. The computer decides. The bonuses are the same."

"And if somebody gets you?"

"The government buries you in Boot Hill free of charge."

"Five thousand dollars is a lot of money," Harold said.

"Oh sure it is, and once dead you're dead for a long time."

"Well, that's true enough," Harold said. "But a man might just get dead anyhow, even if he didn't sign up to kill somebody, and still never get to see five thousand dollars."

"Don't think it's an easy way of making money," Nora cautioned him. "They pay people a lot to join the Hunt here, because that's what brings in the tourist money and keeps Huntworld rich. But there's a pretty high death rate among first-time Hunters. All the advantage is with the regulars."

"Still, even the regulars had to start with their first kill, just like me."

"True enough," Nora said.

"I hear that people come here from all over the world to kill people they don't even know. Is that right?"

"Yes, it is. Weird, isn't it? I read a theory on that in a magazine. It was about what they called the Huntworld Syndrome, whatever that is. Or maybe it was the Huntworld Mentality. They said it was a generalized unconscious death wish in response to population pressure."

"That doesn't make any sense," Harold said. "I thought the world was depopulated or underpopulated or whatever you call it."

"Well, it is, in terms of what the population was a hundred years ago. But there's still too many people trying to share out what's left. And every year there's less. Everything's breaking down, nobody's building new stuff, nobody has any money, not even much get-up-and-go. Except for Hunters, I guess."

"Makes sense. Five thousand dollars is sure a lot of money. I guess I wouldn't mind killing somebody for that. If he had gone into it of his own free will, just like me. I wouldn't mind that."

"Suppose he killed you?" Nora asked.

"Well, I guess that's one of the risks that goes with the job."

"How can you call it a job?"

"Because it *is* a job. Killing people. For five thousand a pop. Only sometimes they get you. I'd call that not too bad a deal."

They finished their dinner, and Harold walked Nora home. At the door Nora said, "Do you want to stay over here, Harold?"

"I thought you'd never ask."

"You can't go on paying hotel prices. I've got a little room in the back you can have. I'll give you a key and you can come and go as you please."

"I'd appreciate it," Harold said. "I've paid up my hotel room for one night, and I guess I'll stay there to keep an eye on my stuff and take another bath. But I'd like to move in tomorrow."

"Come in for a moment." She gave him a key. "Harold, I'm out a lot. You know how it is."

"Don't worry about me, Nora. I'm not judging you, whatever it is you do. I shot a dog on the way down here and put a hole in a guy's shoulder and pretty soon I'll be doing worse than that. That's just how it is."

"Don't get into the Hunt too quick," Nora said. "There's a really high death rate with first-time Hunters."

"But you got to start somewhere."

"That's sure the truth," Nora said, with a certain grimness.

16 • • • • •

Mike Albani parked his white Lamborghini convertible, waved hello to a pretty neighbor with a three-year-old in a baby carriage, and went to his door. He looked both ways out of common caution; it was not unknown for the families of deceased victims to take their revenge upon Spotters even though such action was against both the civil and the moral code. Finding nothing suspicious in the vicinity, he quickly unlocked his door and slipped in.

His wife, Teresa, was in the Florida room watching television. She had on *Mars Colony Diary,* a daily show broadcast direct from Mars Station, picked up by relay stations and sold to the cable networks. Teresa was fascinated by the details of daily life in exotic places. She had a lot of patience. She could sit for hours just watching tomatoes grow in the backyard. You can't get much more patient than that.

"So how did it go today?" Teresa asked.

Albani slumped in his chair. All the flash and flair which he presented to the outside world had drained out of him.

"I gave a guy a lift from the airport. He might decide to Hunt, and if he does he might take me on as his Spotter."

"That's wonderful," Teresa said. "What about the guy you're spotting for now?"

"Jeffries?" He brightened up a little. "He took a day off today. Says he can't Hunt properly with a head cold. But I have a beautiful ambush set up for tomorrow. We're going to get his Victim, don't worry about that."

"Is he any good, this Jeffries?"

"One successful Hunt as a Victim so far. But they say it was pure luck, got the guy with a ricochet."

Teresa sighed. "You can really pick them, can't you?"

"I didn't pick Jeffries. He picked me. I have to Spot for these guys until I get the one who can make a good kill so we can get some bonus money. Don't worry about it, OK?"

Teresa shrugged. Albani poured himself a glass of wine. He was a deeply troubled man with everything going wrong and his life collapsing around him.

Mike Albani was thirty-six years old, originally from Dorchester, Massachusetts. His father, Giancarlo, an immigrant from Castellammare in Italy, worked as a mechanic in Providence before moving to Dorchester. Giancarlo and Maria Albani had six children. Mike's mother worked in a neighborhood laundry on Neponset Avenue. Mike was one of six children. The others were now living in different parts of the United States—the three survivors, that is. Angelo was killed trying to rob a bank in Cheyenne, Wyoming, and Tito died in an auto wreck outside Sioux Falls.

As a kid, Mike had shown talent as an organizer of petty crime. He was doing well for himself in Dorchester and the Boston Southside when one of his gang, Mad Dog Lonnigan, was caught robbing a Thom McAn shoe store in Brookline and turned state's evidence in return for immunity from prosecution. Mike heard about this through his connections, just in time to get out of town. He arrived in Huntworld in 2081.

After a succession of odd jobs he was taken on as an apprentice by Luigi Vanilli, a canny old Spotter from Sicily. When Vanilli was shot to death in a dispute with a neighbor over a pear tree that grew in the neighbor's yard but overhung Vanilli's property, Vanilli's daughter, Teresa, inherited the client list, the white Lamborghini, and the house. Teresa and Mike already had an understanding, and were married soon after.

Mike's first year as a Spotter was marked by brilliant successes. His second kill especially was noted in the record book. And then he had the good luck to be employed by the brilliant killer Julio Sanchez from Costa Rica. Within two years of his arrival in Esmeralda, Albani had everything a man could hope for.

But then Sanchez was killed—it happens even to the best of them sooner or later—and it was all downhill after that. The word around town was that Albani had lost his touch, the fantasy and flair that had made his setups so interesting. It was suggested that he had Spotter's block. Nobody wants to work with an unlucky Spotter. It got so bad Albani had to hang around the airport trying to solicit trade from greenhorns.

In Huntworld, the rise and fall of fortune is fast indeed. Albani was struggling to get back on top. His only client now was Jeffries, an eccentric Englishman who didn't show much promise.

Albani was badly in need of a success. Like Hunters and Victims, Spotters are paid per Hunt, both by their clients and by the state. But if his client gets killed, the Spotter is fined the amount of his bonus plus ten percent for court costs. Albani's last three clients had been unsuccessful. Each failure brought Albani an increasingly heavy fine. Now he stood poised on a razor's edge. If Jeffries made his kill, Albani would be able to stave off doom awhile longer. If Jeffries lost, Albani would be fined again, coming that much closer to being wiped out.

Being wiped out in Huntworld meant being put

through a formal rite of de-emancipation. At the conclusion he would be declared a slave, have all his assets taken by the state, and be assigned a state-chosen job probably on a level with shoveling shit on a hog farm.

Teresa said suddenly, "Michelangelo, let's go back to Dorchester."

Albani shook his head. "There's still a warrant out for me."

"Well, what about somewhere else in America?"

"Starvation on the installment plan? Forget it. I just need one good break. If only I could find another Sanchez."

"Sanchez was very good," Teresa said. "You're right, Sanchez had class, and you had class while you were with him. But he got killed. And after him there was Antonelli."

"Don't remind me."

"Mike, what will we do?"

"Jeffries will make his kill and I'll be on my way back up. Or this new fellow, Harold, will employ me and we will ride to success on his murdering abilities."

"And if not?"

"If all else fails, I will take the Suicide Facility and leave the benefits to you."

"Big talk," Teresa said. "You always threaten suicide when you're feeling depressed."

"I'll do it this time," Albani said, standing up. "I'll do it right now. And then who will you have to complain to?"

Teresa knew it was just a bluff—probably—but it scared her all the same. "No, Albani," she said, her voice trembling, "don't take the suicide option."

"All right," Albani said, sitting down again. "I just wanted you to know that I'm thinking of you."

17 • • • • •

Dear Allan,

Well here I am in Huntworld and I almost got killed on my first day here. Aside from that, I haven't seen much of the Hunting that this place is famous for. I guess I expected people to be running around the streets like in that old movie they made before the Hunt became legal—*Tenth Victim*, that's the one. I do hear what I think is gunfire from time to time, but it's hard to tell for sure. Maybe I just haven't been in the right places at the right time.

This afternoon I ran into one of the people I came over on the airplane with from Miami—a guy named Tex Draza. I guess you'd call him a cowboy only there aren't hardly any cows left anymore even in Texas where he comes from. We stopped off and had a drink together in a saloon called Sloppy Joe's. They claim that this is the original Sloppy Joe's, though I don't know what that's supposed to mean. It was a nice friendly place down near the end of Main Street, and the walls were filled with photos of famous people who have been through there. Draza and I drank Zombies, a very ancient drink that dates back to the twentieth century. It's a mixture of all kinds of rums and a few chemicals, too, and boy, it is potent.

I had been wondering about all the new construction that's going on in town and the flags and banners and stuff they're hanging all over. It seems that I've come here practically on the eve of Esmeralda's biggest holiday. Saturnalia, they call it. Well, it seems that on this day, everybody dresses up in elaborate costumes and there is a great deal of sexual license, though Draza only hinted at this. I'd kinda like to see that.

During Saturnalia, Draza told me, there's parties and parades and floats and sports events and dancing contests and all that, and there's also this custom called Passing the Spot.

The Spot is a small brass cylinder with a red spot on its side. Inside it's got a small but powerful little bomb, strong enough to kill anyone within a foot or so of it. This bomb is armed and ready to be set off by an internal timing device. But nobody knows exactly when the bomb will go off. Sometime during Saturnalia, that's all they know.

But what they do, Allan, if you can believe this, they pass this Spot around from hand to hand, like Russian Roulette only with a bomb instead of a gun. A man or a woman shows how much guts they have by hanging on to the Spot for a while before handing it to someone else. Tourists don't have to take the Spot, but many of them do anyhow. I guess they're like the foreigners who used to run in the streets with the bulls in Pamplona, like Hemingway wrote about.

I saw Nora last night. She looked great. She lives in a picturesque section near the center of the city. I'm staying with her awhile until I can get my own place. The streets where she lives are narrow and winding, and vehicles are forbidden. The place looks so old, what with all the buildings being made of stone and set at funny angles to each other, that you forget it's not old at all. Most of the city was built in the last seventy years.

I like it here. I like how this little city twists and turns and sprawls around. There's always something interesting to look at. It's a happy place, and that's a weird thing to say about a place dedicated to death, but it's true.

I've been checking out this Hunt situation and it looks pretty good. I'll be getting into it soon, after I learn a little more about it. Tell Caleb and the others I'll be sending them some money as soon as I can make some.

I'm writing this from a bar in the downtown area. It's funny, I've just seen someone I know. He's the guy who gave me a lift from the airport the other day. A Spotter. Mike Albani. I'll continue this later.

18 • • • • •

Albani was sitting on a red plush barstool drinking a glass of white wine. He wore a neatly cut blue blazer, gray flannel slacks, and highly polished black loafers. He wore a blue silk ascot around his neck, tucked into his crisp white shirt. His dark handsome face broke into a dazzling smile when Harold came over.

"Harold! Delighted to see you! I hope you've been enjoying yourself on our little island."

"It's a real pretty place," Harold said. "I've been having a fine time."

"What do you think about our Hunt?"

"Seems like an interesting proposition, if you can just keep from getting killed."

"A good Spotter helps you stay alive. Can I get you a drink?'"

"Thanks. I'll take whatever you're having."

"Another white wine, Charlie," Albani said to the white-jacketed bartender.

Harold perched on a barstool next to Albani. "You're not out meeting the planes today?"

"No. What we're getting now is the holiday rush before Saturnalia. Most of these people aren't interested in the fine art of the Hunt. They just want to get drunk, get a woman, make a lot of noise, and afterward be able to tell people how wild they were in Huntworld. There's no harm in it, of course, and I don't look down upon them. But I do somewhat miss the old days."

"What was it like in the old days?" Harold asked.

Albani smiled wistfully. He took a gold-tipped cigarette from a silver case, lit it, exhaled a plume of smoke, then offered the case to Harold. "Go on, try one. It's basically a mixture of Virginia and Yenidje tobaccos treated with a mild mood elevator called Uptime 32. Nothing hallucinogenic, just a lift to the spirits."

Harold accepted a cigarette, lit up, took a small inhalation, coughed it out, tried a smaller one, and found he could stand that. The smoke had an odd spicy-sweet flavor which he found unpleasant at first but then quickly got used to.

"You don't have to hold in the smoke," Albani said. "Don't even bother inhaling. The active ingredients go into the bloodstream through the mucous membranes of the mouth. Quite harmless, nonaddicting, and perfectly legal, of course. But you were asking me about the good old days. As recently as twenty years ago, Hunting was almost a religious ritual. Every head of family would be sure to get in at least one Hunt a year. People used to hire whole families of Spotters back in those days, when money was a little easier to come by. These Spotters were your team, and they were much more than mere employees. They were like family, even though you did have to pay them. The custom was a little like that of noble families during the Renaissance, when every wealthy man had his flock of clients."

"Sounds nice," Harold said.

Albani nodded, a wistful expression in his lustrous brown eyes. "Back then a well-trained Spotter had more work than he could handle. Sometimes a Spotter would make enough from his clients to afford to go into Hunting himself."

"Is it such an expensive practice?" Harold asked. "I thought you just needed a gun."

"It's not the Hunting itself that's so expensive. It's just that if you're at all serious about it, you tend to do it to the exclusion of everything else. Most Hunters find it inconvenient to hold a full-time job. Having to work cuts down on your killing time, ties you to a routine which leaves you vulnerable to surprise attack and ambush. Bad idea, working. We don't do much of it in Huntworld."

"Then how do you live?"

"The government pays a yearly stipend to each registered Hunter based on the tax officer's estimate of how much he might earn if he weren't spending all his time Hunting. Negative income tax, it's called. A very popular feature. And there's also a bonus for each registered kill."

"But how can the government afford all that? It must mean they're supporting half of the population."

"Oh, it's all carefully calculated. Hunting is our biggest tourist draw and our main source of foreign revenue. By Hunting we keep the money coming in, and the government does its best to keep the Hunters and their Spotters in fighting funds. Unfortunately, it's not enough, as I well know."

"You?" Harold said. "You look like you're doing OK."

"One must keep up a front. But I'm actually just barely getting by. Most of my money has been lost in another of Huntworld's practices, one even more addicting than murder. I refer to the king of the vices, gambling."

"Couldn't you stay away from it?" Harold asked.

"Not really. Our gambling laws are unique in the world. Not only is it legal to gamble here, at times it is obligatory."

"The government *makes* you gamble?"

"Most of us need no encouragement. It's all part

of the risk-taking attitude that is at the heart of the Esmeraldan character."

"What happens to the ones who lose?"

"If they lose enough," Albani said, "they go bankrupt."

"And then?"

"For those who reach absolute bankruptcy—the bottom rung, completely tapped out, no money, nowhere they can borrow anymore—such people forfeit their remaining goods and become slaves of the government."

"Slaves!" Harold said. "You can't mean it! There's no slavery in the modern world!"

"Isn't there?" Albani said. He turned to the bartender. "Charles, tell Mr. Erdman about slavery."

"Sure," the bartender said cheerfully. He was a big, moon-faced man, paunchy and bald, wiping red hands on a soiled blue-and-white-check apron. "I can tell you about it from the inside." He held out one hand. "See that ring? That's a government slave ring."

It was a plain black pinkie ring made of some shiny substance—ebony, perhaps—and set with a single small sparkling stone.

"It'll be three years this spring that I became a government slave," Charles said. "Five-card stud, that was my undoing. I've been leased out to the hotel here to help out during the tourist season. The rest of the time I'm a cargo inspector in the government custom service."

Harold didn't know what to say. It didn't seem polite to ask a slave how he felt about slavery. But that was assuming that there was something shameful about slavery. Charles didn't seem to feel that way. Nor did Mike Albani.

'Slavery is necessary in a place like this," Albani said. "Our citizens spend all their time having fun and looking for excitement. There just aren't enough people around to do the serious work of keeping things going. It's even difficult to find people to fill offices in local government. Most of the government work is done by slaves. Slavery is the only way to get people to take care of practical things like public sanitation and building maintenance."

"Weird," said Harold.

"Slavery is actually a pretty good system," Charles said. "You can take all the risks and lead an exciting life without the fear of anything terribly bad happening to you aside from getting killed. The worst that's going to happen is that you'll run through your money and have to work for a living."

"And even then," Albani said, "it's not forever. They start you out on the lowest level, of course— cleaning out the pig farms or working in the salt mines. But with a little luck you can move up to the administrative level. Government slaves in the administration are paid very well, as you might imagine, since they *are* the government and they vote their own salaries. It doesn't take long for a government slave to be able to buy himself free."

"It's all very strange to me," Harold said. "Not that some of it doesn't seem to make some sense. What I find hard to understand is why people who don't need the money risk their lives in this Hunt."

"It does take a certain frame of mind," Albani admitted. "Perhaps you have to live here awhile before you can feel its attractiveness. A lot of people feel that being a good Hunter is better than being a good anything else."

"What does it take to be a good Hunter?"

"Cool nerves and luck. It has very little to do with expertise in weapons, or quick draws, or learning how to sneak around without being seen, or any of that pseudomilitary stuff. The essence of the Hunt is living your natural life in the midst of danger."

"You must get a lot of real aggressive types here."

Albani looked pained. "Not at all. The Hunt is more inclined to favor the subtleties of introversion."

"I don't know if you've convinced me," Harold said. "But this has certainly given me a great deal to think about."

The telephone at the end of the bar rang. The bartender went over to answer it. He spoke for a moment, then called Albani to the phone. Albani went to the phone, spoke briefly, and came back.

"I'd love to go on with our discussion," Albani said. "But alas, duty calls." He looked at his wrist-watch. "I'm due at an ambush in precisely twenty minutes. But I could give you a lift if you're going that way."

"Where is the ambush?" Harold asked. He was smoking another of Albani's cigarettes and feeling light-headed and devil-may-care.

"Oh, it's across town, over toward the Tulip Palace, on the Quatranango Heights, near the zoo. A very pretty section if you haven't seen it already."

"Let's go," Harold said.

19 •••••

The sun rode low in the west, wrapped in the purple clouds of evening. A pinkish glow touched the whitewashed buildings of Esmeralda. The palm fronds along Ocean Boulevard clattered in the rising evening breeze as Harold got into Albani's white convertible.

When you're driving down a palm-lined boulevard on a perfect golden afternoon it's hard to be too worried about what you're going to do when you reach your destination. The ride's the thing, whether it's to a wedding or a wake.

The stiff breeze blowing in from the sea had a savor of salt and iodine in it, and the faint rank smell of kelp piled up on the beaches. Albani drove with firm expertise, but without undue haste, west through the white-and-pink-stucco suburbs of Maldorado and Inchburg. He turned onto a secondary road just outside the city and they began climbing toward the heights of Lansir. There passed roadsigns for the zoo and the miniature rain forest. As they climbed the air became cool and the level plain of Esmeralda was suddenly revealed below them, dotted with farms and pastureland sloping down to the shining sea.

Albani pulled up at the entrance to the zoo. "I could drop you here," Albani said. "It's quite a good zoo, I believe. The only wildebeestes in the Caribbean. There's a bus back to town."

Harold said, "I do want to see the zoo, but I could

go some other time. Would you mind if I came along? I've never been to an ambush."

"Of course, delighted to have you," Albani said.

Albani drove on for a ways, then turned onto a dirt road. The low-slung car banged badly against the high-crowned road. Albani came to a turnout, parked, turned off the engine, and set the emergency brake.

"We'll have to do the next bit on foot," he told Harold.

Albani led them up a narrow footpath and then into the woods. They worked their way through thick underbrush to a final screen of pines, and then they were on a crest overlooking the main road a hundred feet below. On the lip of the crest, directly in front of them, was a V-shaped wooden structure filled with large rocks. The upper part of it rested upon a platform beneath which cogwheel machinery was visible.

"With the turn of a crank," Albani said, "I can drop that whole pile of rocks onto the road. Neat, eh? I had my helpers set it up months ago. People chase people along predictable routes. A good Spotter anticipates.'"

"What's supposed to happen?" Harold asked.

"A car will be coming along this way shortly," Albani said. "The Victim will be in it—a Mr. Draza from Texas."

"Hey," Harold said, "I met him coming over on the plane."

"He visits Esmeralda every year," Albani said. "This is his sixth successful Hunt, I believe. And his last. When his car reaches that milepost there, I will drop these rocks into the roadway in front of him, blocking his passage. Mr. Draza will get out. While he is trying to figure out where we are, his Hunter— Mr.

Scott Jeffries, my employer—will drill him from a vantage point alongside the road."

"Sounds a little complicated," Harold said. "Isn't there any simpler way to get the guy?"

Albani looked scornful. "Many other ways, no doubt. But ambushes of this sort are traditional. They also have the virtue of keeping Spotters employed. Now I'll just make sure everything is all right."

Albani drew a small radio out of his pocket and extended its long whip antenna. "Mr. Jeffries, are you in position?"

The radio crackled. A man's thin high voice said, "Yes, I'm in position and ready. Is he coming?"

Albani scanned the road. "Yes, and right on time!"

From that height the approaching silver car was small indeed. Albani leaned forward, his hand on the trigger of the rock-dropping mechanism. Harold stood a few feet behind him, taking in the scene. A flash of light caught the corner of his eye. It had come from the wooded hillside behind and to his right. Harold turned. There was the flash again. And then he made out something—a shape—moving in the trees.

Harold didn't know who it was or what it meant, but suddenly he was shocked into alertness, his pulses hammering. He shouted, "Get down!" and swept Albani off his feet. A split second later he heard the sharp flat crack of a high-powered rifle. A bullet slammed into the rock cradle where Albani had been standing.

Harold started to get up. Albani pulled him back down. There were four more shots, evenly spaced. From far away Harold could hear the sound of the car, a high thin buzz which grew louder, then fainter as it passed the failed ambush and went on.

"What do we do now?" Harold asked, lying flat on the ground.

"We wait. It's obvious there's a Spotter up there in the woods somewhere. He shouldn't be shooting at us like that. It's not the regular form, and certainly shows no professional courtesy to me."

"Can't you shoot back?"

"No gun. Spotters aren't supposed to carry them. And even if I had one, I wouldn't break the rules just because some untrained lout does so. Just stay down. Jeffries will be up here soon and the Spotter will go away."

"Won't he try to kill Jeffries?"

"Certainly not. Spotters are not permitted to kill Hunters."

Within minutes Jeffries had scrambled up the hillside, his rifle at high port. He was a small, ivory-skinned man with plastered black hair, a small mustache, and a brown mole above his long upper lip. "Are you all right, Albani?" he asked.

"I'm fine," Albani said. "But obviously, I have been Spotted. And worse than that, anticipated. Me, Albani! Frankly, I'm mortified."

"Don't take it too hard, old fellow," Jeffries said. "Sometimes one simply has an off day."

"But I ruined your kill," Albani said, wringing his hands.

"Think nothing of it. I wasn't really in the mood today. Feeling a bit peckish. My doctor tells me I've been inhaling too much cordite. Never mind. Who is this?"

"This is a friend, Mr. Harold Erdman, from America. He saved my life."

"Good show," Jeffries said. "Wouldn't want to lose you, Albani. I must be getting back now. Good to meet you, Erdman. We'll get the fellow next time, eh, Albani?"

"You can count on it!"

"Give me a call when you've set him up again. Something in the city, if possible. I really don't fancy climbing up and down these hills. Good to meet you, Erdman." Jeffries turned and went back down the hillside.

Albani was silent on the drive back to the city. He pulled up in front of the Estrella and said, "Harold, you did me a good turn. How did you know that fellow was there?"

"I think I caught a glint of light off his telescopic lens," Harold said.

"But at that distance, how did you know it was a telescopic lens? Never mind. You're quick. You'd do well at our game. Look, how would you like to come to a party tomorrow night?"

"A party?" Harold said. "Whose party?"

"It's the Hunt Jubilee Ball," Albani said. "Given once a year just before Saturnalia, and with a very restricted and exclusive guest list. All the top Hunters are there, of course, and the usual array of movie people, rock stars, senators, that sort of people. It would be something to tell your friends."

Harold said, "I don't have any plans for the evening. But could I bring a friend?'"

"No problem." He took out his billfold and gave Harold an engraved invitation for two. "It's at the Hunt Academy. Come around ten o'clock. That's when it starts getting lively."

20 • • • • •

Flight 461 from Atlanta was almost an hour late getting into Esmeralda, and Louvaine Daubray was fuming. He was in the middle of a Hunt that was proving rather grueling, and his cousin Jacinth Jones, in her senior year at Bennington, had decided at the last moment to spend her interterm vacation with him.

Jacinth always picked inconvenient times to come visiting. She had decided at the last moment to come last year, and Louvaine was sure it was all the extra fuss, having to fix up the spare bedroom for her, that had thrown him off his stride and resulted in his making a kill so sloppy that he had been criticized not only in the newspapers but also on the usually sympathetic *Huntworld Show*, where the m.c., Gordon Philakis himself, had referred to it as involuntary vivisection and added that Louvaine had shown all the grace of a horse falling on a mole.

It was true that his victim that year had worn thick spectacles, and that Louvaine's attempt to cut him down with a saber from horseback had been successful only because his horse panicked and fell on top of the guy. Louvaine didn't like to think about it. It had been the beginning of his run of bad luck.

He had considered sending Souzer, his Spotter, out to meet Jacinth, but he knew that Jacinth would be offended and would probably mention it to his mother. Louvaine's mother, living alone in Sharon,

Connecticut, since the death of her husband, controlled the family trust that kept Louvaine in funds.

Sarah Daubray was opposed to the entire Huntworld philosophy. She had said on several occasions that only the poor should kill each other, since the wealthy were too valuable to sacrifice. Louvaine, however, was a liberal; he believed anyone had the right to kill anyone else, rich or poor.

Sarah Daubray's sister was Ellen Jones, Jacky's mother. If Jacinth reported home that Louvaine had been too busy trying to kill someone to meet her at the airport . . . well, it might not make any difference, but still, why take chances with something important like money?

So here he was sitting in the airport observation tower and chain-smoking, and here came the plane at last, swooping down out of the clear blue Caribbean sky trailing its dark cloud of jet smoke.

Jacinth came through the gate. She was twenty years old, slender and of medium height, with stylishly short sleek black hair, pretty features, thin crimson lips.

"Louvaine, darling, how great! I was so looking forward to seeing you again!"

Jacinth didn't especially like Louvaine, but she always enjoyed staying in Huntworld, especially at Saturnalia time, and Louvaine had a super apartment right near Central Square.

"Jacinth, I'm delighted." He always called her by her full name. "If you don't mind, love, we'll get right back to the apartment. I'm right in the middle of a Hunt; you know how it is. I'll have someone pick up your luggage."

Louvaine Daubray was thirty-four years old, of medium height, with thin ash-blond hair and eyebrows so fair they were almost invisible. His father had been a successful stockbroker in New Haven,

Connecticut, and, after his retirement, a notable Hunter in Esmeralda with twelve kills to his credit before a Turkish Hunter disguised as a waiter blew him all over the antipasto wth a Sten gun.

Louvaine's mother, Sarah, a society woman proud of her one-eighth Iroquois blood, had stayed in Sharon, Connecticut, to administer the family trust and buy and sell antique stores, a hobby she had always wanted to pursue. Louvaine had a large and beautiful apartment in downtown Esmeralda and a little villa out on the island. He had everything a man could wish for except the satisfaction that comes from doing a job well.

He showed Jacinth her room and sat down at his worktable. He loved playing with his guns. He had three that he was especially fond of: a Webley-Martin .303, a Beretta double-barreled derringer firing a .44 slug, and a long-barreled .22 target pistol. Several more handguns lay on his worktable, stripped down, and there were others in an ebony rack on the wall. There was a smell of machine oil in the air.

Jacinth Jones came back into the living room. She sprawled on the couch with her stockinged feet in the air, a cigarette smoldering in an ashtray on a side table beside her. From where he sat, Louvaine could see only her sleek cap of black hair and her stockinged feet kicking idly as she read a fashion magazine she had picked up on the plane.

The telephone rang. Louvaine reached for it, but Jacinth picked up the extension on the little end table near her head.

"Sally? Darling, how are you? Yes, I've just arrived, isn't it exciting? Of course I'm going to the Hunt Ball. What are you wearing?"

Louvaine was making ferocious faces at her and gesturing at the telephone.

"I'd better talk to you later," Jacinth said. "Louvaine

needs the phone. See you later." She hung up and said to Louvaine, "All right now?"

"I'm sorry," Louvaine said. "But you know I'm waiting to hear from my Spotter."

"Are you a Hunter or a Victim this time?"

"A Hunter. My Victim is a Fred C. Harris."

"Never heard of him."

"He's not a local. Comes from New Jersey. This is his third Hunt. Very quick little man with silver hair. In the movie business, I believe. According to what I've been able to learn he's got some pretty cute moves."

"Are you still using Otto Spangler for your Spotter?"

Louvaine shook his head. "He died in a car accident last month fulfilling his Reckless Driving Obligation."

"I've never been able to understand that custom."

"Not all customs have to have a reason."

"Who are you using now?"

"Ed Souzer. Did you ever meet him? Fat man with a head like a melon, comes from Key West?"

Jacinth shook her head. "He sounds neither familiar nor interesting. Why don't you use Tom Dreymore? You always spoke so highly of him."

"He's busy this week."

"Too busy for you? I find that hard to believe, considering what you pay?"

"Tom doesn't need the work. He's been very successful of late. I tried to get him, but he was always out and never returned my calls. I think he's avoiding me."

"Why would he do that?"

"You've been away, Jacinth. You weren't here for my last Hunt."

"You were just setting it up when I went back to

Bennington. What happened? You got the guy, didn't you?"

"Of course I did. Otherwise I wouldn't be sitting here now, would I?"

"Then what was the trouble?"

"The Hunting Referees said it was an inelegant kill. Just because I had to finish the guy off with a shotgun."

"There's nothing in the rules against that, is there?"

"Of course not. It's perfectly legal. But they got angry because I blew the guy all over the front of the Hospitality Building just when a load of tourists were passing. There were several tour cancellations. But why blame me? I mean, what did they expect? If people are squeamish, they shouldn't come here at all. God knows it's no secret what we do in Hunt-world."

"There's no penalty for making an inelegant kill, is there?"

"No. The Huntworld code states explicitly that you can put your man down in any way you wish. But there are style points, and there's the Warrior of the Year Award for best kill, and there's the Big Payoff. I never get any of those."

"Poor Louvaine," Jacinth said.

"Look, it's no joke. You weren't here for my first kills. People said they had never seen anything like it. I used nothing but the .22 target pistol then, and I could shoot with either hand. I used to put those guys away before they knew what was hitting them. People predicted I'd win the higher honors. I was always being written up in the magazines and inter- viewed on television. But then something started going wrong. I was just as good as ever on the practice range. But in actual combat I was tightening up, missing the head shot, missing the heart shot, damn near getting myself killed. Jacinth, this really has me worried. It's not just for myself. It's the family name."

"Maybe you'll have a good one this time out," Jacinth said.

"I need it badly. I've been thinking of seeing a psychiatrist about this problem. I've never told anyone that but you. Sometimes I think I'm just getting old."

"Old? At thirty-four? Don't be silly." She thought Louvaine was in fact getting a little long in the tooth, but she kept that opinion to herself.

"I don't feel old," Louvaine said. "But still—"

Just then the telephone rang. Louvaine grabbed it, listened, said, "Right, Souzer," and hung up. He slipped on his special jacket with the built-in weapons pockets. "I really must go."

"Can I come too?"

"No, I'll see you later."

"Oh, come on, Louvaine, I've been gone so long, it would really be like a homecoming to watch you make your kill. Maybe I'd bring you luck."

"Absolutely not," Louvaine said. "Women are bad luck on a Hunt. I'll tell you all about it when I get back."

He hurried out the door. Jacinth had never seen Louvaine so nervous. She hoped he'd do well this time. He could get into a terrible temper when he made a sloppy kill. A lot of men were like that.

21 • • • • •

Louvaine met Souzer in Blake's Coffee Shop near the downtown aquarium. Souzer apologized for the delay, explaining that the Victim, Mr. Fred C. Harris of Summit, New Jersey, had dawdled longer over his lunch than anticipated, and then had crossed Souzer up by going back to his hotel for a nap. He had just reappeared, rested and freshly shaved, a jolly little man with a neatly trimmed mustache flecked with gray.

"Where is he now?" Louvaine asked.

"Across the street in the bookstore. He goes in there every day. He only bought a book once, though."

"What kind of a book?"

Souzer took a notepad out of his hip pocket and consulted it. "The 2091 edition of *The Shooter's Bible.*"

"That figures. How's he armed?"

Souzer turned a page in the notepad. "He's got a Ruger Redhawk DA .44 Magnum in a Mexican leather shoulder holster, and a Taurus Model 85 .38 in a hip holster. He also has a replica Bowie knife strapped to his left leg."

"You're thorough, Souzer, I'll say that for you. Did you happen to learn the color of his underwear?"

Souzer flipped through the pages of his notepad. "I've probably got it here somewhere."

"Never mind," Louvaine said. "Did you get his target practice scores?"

"He closes his eyes and squeezes."

"That's what I like to hear," Louvaine said. Then

he frowned. "But blind squeezers do get lucky sometimes."

"Not this guy," Souzer said. "He's a walking death wish if I ever saw one. A murder looking for a place to happen. I'd suggest Plan A, the direct approach. Get behind him just after he leaves the bookstore. Let him see you by the time you get to Fairfax. He'll turn into that alley between Sofrito and Main that goes past the back of Shultz's Diner. That's where he thinks he's going to get you. That's where you get him."

"It's got to be a good kill," Louvaine said, more to himself than to Souzer.

"You'll have everything going for you," Souzer said. "A nice narrow alley, a spotlight I've set up to shine in his eyes, and that special little surprise when he gets to the diner door. It's really a beautiful setup. Which gun did you decide to use?"

"The Widley," Louvaine said, taking the autoloader out of a shoulder holster. "It's heavy, fifty-one ounces with the six-inch barrel, and it ruins the line of my sports jacket. But it's damned accurate and carries a fourteen-round clip."

"What are you loaded with?"

"Winchester 9-millimeter Magnums. And I'm also carrying a Smith & Wesson Model 59 just in case."

"It's good to have a backup," Souzer agreed. "Hey, he's coming out now!"

Fred C. Harris came out of the bookshop and walked briskly down Main. Louvaine slid the Widley out of its holster and into his hand and left the coffee shop. He walked rapidly until he was about twenty feet behind Harris, then slowed. The Widley felt good in his hand, solid, dependable. Louvaine thought of it as precision death at the end of his hand. He thumbed off the safety and jacked a round into the chamber. Harris was just ahead of him, a tempting target, but

Louvaine couldn't shoot yet; there were too many people in the way and the penalties for hitting bystanders were severe.

Harris had spotted him now and had his gun out, but he was in an awkward position to use it and he kept on going, hurrying now, breaking into a run, his white hair flying, dodging around to keep people between him and Louvaine. Louvaine was also running, pulses hammering in his temples, his system flooded with adrenaline, floating along on Hunter's High when the world goes into slow motion and you're never going to die.

Harris slipped into the alley just as Souzer had said he would. Souzer had deduced Harris's plan. It was to lure Louvaine into this alley and then to slip through the back door into Shultz's Diner. There was a slit cut in that door just big enough for a gun barrel. The door itself was steel-plated. Harris was figuring that he'd have Louvaine dead to rights then, himself crouched down behind steel plating with Louvaine targeted in the alley. Some idiot cut-rate Spotter must have sold him on that one. It showed the crap you got when you didn't pay for the very best.

Harris reached the back door of the diner as Louvaine turned into the alley. Harris wrenched at the door, but it was locked, of course; Souzer had seen to that. When Harris touched the doorknob, it set off a switch that activated a powerful searchlight, also set up by Souzer. The powerful beam hit Harris right in the eyes, and the little man realized he'd been had. He was trying blind to bring his gun up to firing position when Louvaine stopped, took a firm two-handed stance, and began firing.

Harris got off one wild shot. Then he stumbled and fell backward over a garbage can.

Louvaine, riding the Hunter's High, was firing what he thought was a couple of times, and he knew that he was aiming high. He tried to correct while still firing and suddenly he was clicking on an empty chamber and damned if he hadn't fired off the whole fourteen-shot clip.

He fumbled in his pocket for another clip. He was bathed in cold sweat. He couldn't believe he'd triggered off the whole clip just like that. Harris had him dead to rights now. All the little clown had to do was poke his gun out from behind that garbage can and blast away.

But Harris wasn't moving. By the time Louvaine had found an extra clip and loaded it, it was apparent that Harris was dead and that Louvaine had broken quite a lot of windows on both sides of the alley.

So he had won again. Louvaine closed his eyes and stood perfectly still as the speed and energy drained out of him. When he opened his eyes again there was somebody in the alley with him. It took Louvaine a moment to recognize the khaki hat and blue enamel insignia that marked a Kill Checker.

The Checker bent over the garbage can with his clipboard and pen, ready to take down the important data concerning the decedent's status in the Hunt.

"How many times did I get him?" Louvaine asked.

"You didn't hit him once," the Checker said. "There's not a mark on him."

"You're kidding," Louvaine said. "He's dead, isn't he?"

"Sure he's dead. But you didn't kill him. Look for yourself."

Louvaine looked. Fred C. Harris from Summit, New Jersey, had that oddly peaceful expression on his face that dead Hunters so often assume in their final moments.

The Checker straightened up. "Looks like he fell

over that garbage can and broke his neck. People don't realize how easy it is to break your neck when you fall backward over a cylindrical object. I'll have to report this as death through natural causes."

"Wait a minute," Louvaine said. "You can't write that in your report."

"Why can't I?"

"Because I won't get credit for the kill."

"I mark 'em like I see 'em," the Checker said, wetting the stub of his pencil.

Louvaine put his gun back in its holster. His hand went into his pocket and came out with that other great weapon—money. The Checker looked at the money hungrily, but he shook his head.

"I can't write that you shot him. There's no blood. Somebody might ask me about that. I could get into a lot of trouble."

"I can take care of the blood right now," Louvaine said, taking out the Widley and aiming at Harris. "He won't care—can't feel a thing."

"Too late," the Checker said. "We got company."

An elderly man in Bermuda shorts and a white-haired woman, presumably his wife, in a violently colored Mother Hubbard, were standing a few feet away snapping their cameras, first at the corpse and then at Louvaine and the Checker and then at each other.

"Tourists," the Checker said. "They're a nuisance, but what would we do without them?"

Louvaine glared at them until they went away. Then he pressed some bills into the Checker's hand. "Whatever you write, try to make me look good."

The Checker nodded, pocketed the bills, thought for a moment, then wrote, "Dead of busted vertebrae sustained while trying to escape certain death at the hands of his Hunter, Mr. Louvaine Daubray."

It wasn't great, but it was enough to get Louvaine

the standard acknowledgment of a successful Hunt. He got the usual bonus, too. But he went home to his apartment feeling discouraged and disgusted with himself. Jacinth was out. He sat in his darkened living room and brooded. How could he have missed with fourteen shots?

He turned on the evening Hunt news. Gordon Philakis of *The Huntworld Show* was running down the day's kills. When he came to Louvaine's he said, "As long as his victim slips, no one notices that Louvaine Daubray is also slipping. Maybe next time his Hunter won't be so obliging."

That was unspeakably vile of Philakis, and Louvaine turned off the television in a fury. Damn it, he was as good as he'd ever been. Better, in fact. He was just having a bad run. He determined that his next Hunt would prove his worth once and for all. In the next Hunt he would kill with unmatchable style. He would set it up so there'd be no mistake. He could afford the best. It was really a matter of finding a more cooperative Victim.

22 • • • • •

Hunter Trials were held every day between nine and four in the Hunt Academy Annex, a low concrete building at the rear of the Hunt Academy. Nora insisted on going with Harold as far as the entrance.

"Look, Harold," she said, "are you sure you want to do this? Once you pass your Trials you're in the Hunt and you can't change your mind. The computer will send you the name of your first opponent within a few days. They won't let you leave the island until you've killed him or he . . . you know."

"I know all that, Nora," Harold said. "I came here to Hunt and make some money, and that's what I'm going to do."

"I've got some friends in this place," Nora said. "I'm sure I could get you a job as a bartender. The tips are really good. You could do all right."

Harold shook his head. "I didn't come all this way to tend bar."

"I don't want to see you get killed!" She clung to him for a moment. There were tears in her blue eyes. Harold hugged her and then stepped back.

"You'd better wait for me back at the apartment. I'll come straight back when I get through here. Tonight we're going to a party."

"What party?"

"Albani said it's the Hunt Jubilee Ball. Supposed to be something special."

"The Jubilee Ball? It's the event of the year! Oh,

Harold, how exciting! But I don't have anything to wear."

"You'll find something," Harold said. "See you later." He kissed her lightly and went into the building.

An official named Mr. Baxter helped Harold with the paperwork. Baxter was a very large fat man who looked like he was about to give birth to a watermelon. He had fuzzy black hair and he wore tiny glinting spectacles. When Harold had completed the forms he led him through a door marked HUNTER TRIALS and down a corridor to a large room lit with overhead fluorescents. At the far end of the room was a brightly painted doorway marked FUNHOUSE TRIALS ENTRANCE.

"That's where you go," Baxter said. "Right through that doorway and follow the corridors. There's only one way to go, so you can't get lost. You can't turn back, either, once you're inside."

"What do I do inside?"

"Whatever you have to do to defend yourself. You'll need this." From a rack on one side of the room he selected a long-handled sledgehammer and gave it to Harold.

"When you come out the other side—assuming nothing goes wrong, of course—I'll be waiting for you."

Harold nodded, hefted the sledgehammer, and looked at the doorway. "What happens in there?"

"Various things," Baxter said. "I'm not permitted to be any more specific than that."

"And this is the only weapon I'm allowed?"

"Correct."

"When do I get the Hunter's bonus?"

"Immediately after the Trials. If you're wounded during your run but are still considered repairable, the money will be applied to your hospital bills. If you're killed the money will go to the beneficiary you indicated on the forms."

Harold had named Nora as his beneficiary. "How often do people get killed in this Trial Run?" he asked.

"As often as we want," Mr. Baxter said.

"I beg your pardon?"

"Statistically, I mean. We never tamper with individual Trials."

"Then what do you mean by statistically?"

"You should have read the brochure," Baxter said. "The Huntworld Council sets the number of Hunters and Victims who may safely contest in the city at any one time. If we let too many people fight at the same time, the result would be an unmanageable chaos. This is how we control the number of fighters, by setting the degree of difficulty of the Trials Course in response to the demand or lack of demand for Hunters."

"I think I see," Harold said. "How high is the degree of difficulty now?"

"Point seven oh two five."

"Is that high?"

"Not in comparison with three years ago," Baxter said.

"That's good."

"But higher than any year since. Your run will be recorded on videotape, by the way. You can watch your own performance tonight on the evening news, assuming it goes all right. You'd better get started."

Harold entered the Funhouse.

He stood inside the entrance for a moment to let his eyes get accustomed to the dark. The door clanged shut behind him. He leaned back against it. It had locked automatically. He had expected that.

He could make out the hum of the cameras from somewhere above him. A pale luminescence came from the walls. The corridor went ahead for a dozen feet, then turned sharply left. He could hear someone giggling. It was a scratchy giggle: recorded.

He moved on, gripping the sledgehammer firmly. Why a sledgehammer?

He heard a flapping noise above and behind him and whirled and ducked instinctively. Something with short broad wings and a long beak swept past him, turned, and came at him again. He could see that it was some sort of mechanical bird with blinking red eyes and stainless-steel beak and talons. Cute but clumsy. He knocked it down with the sledge and trampled it underfoot. There was a tinkling sound as fragile components snapped.

He continued down the corridor. The next thing he heard was a wet snuffling sound, coming toward him out of the darkness. It sounded like a bear, but that was impossible; there weren't any bears left except in zoos. Another windup toy, he thought.

When it came around the corner he saw that it was a composite creature with a goat's body, a lion's head, and a serpent's tail. It was only later that he learned this was a reconstruction of the fabled Chimera of Greek myth.

The Chimera was more trouble than the mechanical bird. Its microcomputer brain seemed to have a few more circuits or something. It dodged and darted and breathed a blowtorch blast of fire at him. Harold backed away, anticipating more trouble behind him. It wasn't long in coming. From the other side came a monster scorpion, the sort of thing they used to show in old Japanese science fiction films.

Harold sidestepped the scorpion and gave it a tap with his sledgehammer, not enough to destroy it, just enough to send it careening into the Chimera. The two big toys swiped and cut at each other and Harold got around them and continued down the corridor.

Next came the simulated rats and bats, and they were unpleasant but not especially dangerous. He cut a way for himself through the critters, taking a few bites here and there but coming through in good shape.

He was feeling pretty confident by now. Maybe overconfident. The next one almost got him. A warrior machine dressed in black from head to toe dropped down from the ceiling and landed in front of him. Harold backed up and almost got decapitated by the warrior's swinging broadsword. He regained his balance and swung the sledgehammer. He was lucky enough to catch the end of the warrior's sword, driving the machine into the wall. Before it could recover Harold sledged it to bits.

He turned down the next corridor, fired up now and ready for anything. He found daylight ahead. He was at the end of the course, and Mr. Baxter was standing there, making notes on a clipboard.

"How'd I do?" Harold asked.

"Well enough," Baxter said. "But it was an easy course. The Trial standards have been set real low this year."

"Then why did you give me that scare talk before?"

"To test your nerve a little, now, at the very beginning. We don't want you to even consider dropping out of the Hunt once you're in it."

"Do people do that?" Harold asked.

"Of course. Some people think they can sign up for the Hunt, pick up the bonus money, and get away quick."

"What's to prevent them?" Harold asked.

"Our police force, of course. No one who signs up for a Hunt gets off Esmeralda until he's finished it."

Harold went back to the main room with Mr. Baxter. There he was given a plastic identity tag to be worn at all times, giving his status as a fully accredited Hunter. He was told to await notification of his first Hunt. He could expect to receive it within a week, maybe a few days if the Hunt computer wasn't down again. Mr. Baxter also gave him a Huntworld replica of a P38 Luger to start his career with, but Harold declined that. His Smith & Wesson was good enough for him. It fit his hand nice and he was used to it.

He also got a check for two thousand dollars. As soon as he endorsed it, Mr. Baxter changed it for him into twenty crisp hundred-dollar bills. Harold left the Hunter Trials Annex and went to the post office. He wired one thousand dollars to Caleb Ott in Keene Valley, New York, and then he went to find Nora and get ready for the party.

23 • • • • •

Albani met his Hunter, Jeffries, downtown in a cigar store near the courthouse. Jeffries looked slightly more alert than usual. That meant he was ready for action.

Albani said, "My informants tell me your Victim comes this way every day. He always has lunch at the same place. That's it across the street; the Alamo Chili House. He claims it's the only food he can stand."

"What sort of food is it?" Jeffries asked.

"Beans and hot sauce," Albani said, "and tough beef."

"And he eats that on purpose?"

"He's from Texas," Albani said. "Texans are different—they can't live long without their native cuisine."

"And how, exactly, do I get him?"

"This guy is pretty cute," Albani said. "After lunch he comes out of the Alamo—always with a toothpick in his mouth—walks down the block, and goes to the Longhorn Bar just down the street for a beer."

"What brand does he drink?"

"Is that important?"

"It might give me an insight into his character."

"He drinks imported Sudetenland Pilsner."

"Ah. That means he's more sophisticated than he may seem at first glance. That's a very important point to remember, Albani. Go on, what's your plan?"

"After having his beer, your Victim walks back to

his hotel. He has on these trick sunglasses that let him see behind him."

"That's bad," Jeffries said.

"No, it's good. The glasses give him a sense of false security. I've calculated that when he reaches the corner of Northrup and the Mall, just as he makes his turn into Sedgwick, there's a blind spot. It's a trick of the afternoon lighting."

"How large a blind spot?"

"Just big enough for you to stand in, Mr. Jeffries. You'll be behind him and to his left. He carries his gun for a right-handed draw. He'll pass within ten feet of you. It's an easy shot."

"Sounds good," Jeffries said. "What sort of weapon is he carrying?"

"A Colt .357 Magnum in a shoulder holster and a five-and-a-half-inch H&R Model 6B6 in an ankle holster."

"A lot of firepower there."

"The idea is not to let him use it on you."

"You're sure about this blind spot?"

"Of course I'm sure. I've made a chalk mark on the sidewalk. Stand right there and he can't see you as he comes by."

"Sounds good," Jeffries said. "Yes, very good indeed. I think this is going to be a good one." He checked the chambers of his Mossberg Abilene .44 Magnum. "I'm ready."

"Wait till he comes out of the Alamo. OK, go!"

Jeffries smoothed back his hair, put the Mossberg in his pocket, and walked out onto the street. He rounded the corner, Albani trailing behind, and took up his station at the indicated place. The Victim, noticeable by his cowboy hat and high-heeled boots, came out of the Alamo, turned to the left just as expected, and walked down the street. He turned the corner. Jeffries let him pass and raised his gun.

At that moment the pavement blew up beneath him.

Albani rushed over. He couldn't believe it. What had happened? There was Jeffries, or what was left of him, smeared out along the broken pavement. The Victim was taking a long thin black cigar out of his pocket, biting off the end, and lighting it. There was the sound of a siren. A car with the official Huntworld seal pulled up and a Kill Checker got out.

"Your name?" the Checker said to the Hunter.

"Tex Draza," the Hunter said.

"You sure leave a mess," the Checker said. "What did you use on this guy?"

"Antipersonnel mine under the pavement."

Albani came up. "That's not allowed. Random killing devices are specifically prohibited under Huntworld law."

"This wasn't any random device," Draza said. "It was keyed to the Hunter's body signature."

"Never heard of that before," the Checker said. "But how did you know this guy was your Hunter?"

"People give themselves away in many little ways," Draza said, and winked. The Checker knew that some unscrupulous Victims were not above paying out large bribes to the right officials in order to learn the names and identities of their Hunters. It made killing them so much easier. He had no proof of this, however; otherwise it would have cost Draza a *really* big bribe.

"Looks like everything's in order," the Checker said.

"'I protest!" Albani said.

The Checker shook his head. "Seems legal enough to me. You were this guy's Spotter?" He indicated the mess on the pavement.

"Well, yes," Albani said. "That is, I was advising

him. I warned him that this wasn't a good setup, but no, Mr. Know-It-All, he had to do it his way. I can't be held responsible for this, officer."

"Take it up with the Adjudication Board," the Spotter said. "Looks like a legal kill to me."

Albani walked away. He was feeling really rotten. He hated the way outsiders with newfangled schemes were coming into Huntworld and changing the entire character of the Hunt. Something ought to be done about it. Now he had another fine to face. This had really turned out to be a rotten day. Thank God there was the Hunt Jubilee Ball tonight. He planned to get drunk and forget his troubles.

24 • • • • •

Nora listened to the story of the Trial Run and felt happy for Harold. It was nice that a boy from her hometown was doing well. And the bonus money was helpful, too. Harold insisted on pulling out two hundred dollars and giving it to her, despite her protests.

"Put in on the rent," Harold told her. "Don't worry, there's more where that came from. After my first kill I get another bonus."

"It's a tough way to earn money," Nora said.

"No, it's an easy way. It's just that everything can come to a screeching halt if things don't go right. But it's still a lot better than what's back home. Listen, Nora, I've worked hard and now I want to celebrate. What about that Jubilee Party?"

"Just give me a moment to change," Nora said.

It took a lot more than a moment, but when she came out of her bedroom Nora looked lovely in a white evening gown and a synthetic fur wrap and her hair done up fancy.

"How do I look?"

"Lady, you look plenty good," Harold said. "By the way, what is this Hunt Jubilee Ball?"

"It's just about the most important social event of the Esmeraldan year. The Jubilee Ball marks the beginning of the Saturnalia season."

"Well," Harold said, "a party's always fun."

"This one especially. They serve wonderful food,

all the liquor you can drink, and every sort of drug known to man."

"I don't go in much for drugs," Harold said. "Except for a little weed now and then."

"You don't have to use any. I'm just telling you what they've got."

"Fair enough. Will I need some new clothes?" He'd had his serge suit cleaned and pressed, but it still didn't look right.

"I've still got Johnson's things here," Nora said. "He was a little shorter than you but big in the chest. The shirts and jackets ought to fit. And maybe I can let down the pants."

"Hell, why don't I just go out and buy a suit?"

"You save your money, Harold Erdman," Nora said, mock-scolding. "You're going to need new weapons, and a Spotter."

"I've seen a lot of fancy firearms around here," Harold said, "but my old Smith & Wesson is plenty good enough for me. As for Spotters, I met this guy named Albani, told me he was a really good Spotter. Looked like he was in need of work. Probably works cheap."

The Jubilee Ball was held in the Mayor's Palace adjoining the Hunt Academy. Uniformed attendants parked the cars of the arriving guests and opened the doors of taxis. The palace had a lot of windows, and they were all glowing with light. Harold looked a little confined and uncomfortable in Johnson's white tuxedo, but he was still a large and impressive figure as they left their taxi and entered the palace.

Nora knew a lot of people and soon was in conversation with a group of her friends. Harold wandered around on his own, uncomfortable in the tuxedo but feeling good. A waiter came by with drinks on a tray and offered him one. Harold took it. It was colored green, but it didn't taste like crème de menthe. Much later he found out it was a Green Devil—a coconut-and-pineapple-juice concoction laced with a new cinnamon-flavored Spanish amphetamine. The mood elevators in the drink began working on him at once, and Harold went from feeling good to feeling very good indeed.

Wherever he went there was a great press of smartly dressed people, several orchestras, buffets, and an inexhaustible supply of servants passing around trays of weird-looking drinks. Harold took another Green Devil and admired the way the chandeliers cast highlights on the women's powdered shoulders. He listened to the babble of conversation but could make little out of it. People seemed to have a strange way of expressing themselves here.

And then he found himself in conversation with a very pretty girl with a shining helmet of black hair. She was wearing a red sheath dress that revealed her spendid shoulders and the upper portions of her fine small bosom. Her name was Jacinth.

"Huntworld is the world's escape valve," Jacinth was saying. "Drives not acted out will surface inappropriately. That simple psychological law is reason enough for the existence of Huntworld."

"That's just what I thought," Harold said.

"Don't play dumb," she said merrily. "It's well known that the cluster of emotions that we signalize by such terms as hunting, killing, defending, and the like require constant stimulation for a healthy personal and social life. Everybody knows that."

"Oh, sure," Harold said.

"It's obvious," she went on, "that the emotions in modern man are atrophied. For many centuries, hunting wild animals acted as a substitute for personal violence. But then populations expanded and urban centers increased in size and density. The animals all got killed off. And then the wars stopped and man was left without anything violent to do. Huntworld filled the killing gap."

"That's amazing," Harold said. "Where did you learn all that stuff?"

"At Bennington."

"Must be quite a place."

The party was at its full fury. The air was filled with blue and yellow smoke from various narcotic substances. A pounding music was playing over gigantic speakers, so loud that Harold could feel it vibrating in his bones. Esmeraldans rated a party on how much noise it made and how much of a fool you were able to make of yourself.

Harold hadn't been doing his bit on that last score. He never drank much, and he knew he was out of his depth in this drug stuff. So he was holding himself in check, even though his head was whirling. He had to bend very far over to hear what Jacinth was saying to him. His ear was in close proximity to her finely carved lips. He could feel her small sharp breasts pressed against him by the movements of the crowd.

Then someone pulled Jacinth away from him and Harold saw a young man in his late twenties or early thirties standing in front of him. He was slim, haughty, blond, with gray eyes and handsome irritable features.

"Jacinth," he said, "if you're quite through licking this man's ear or whatever it is you are doing with it, Tom and Mandy have reserved a table for us on the second level."

"I was just telling him some of the latest theories on the Hunt," Jacinth said. "Harold, this is my cousin Louvaine."

"Pleased to meetcha," Harold said, holding out his hand.

Louvaine looked at it as if he were being offered a

wet fish. He looked Harold up and down. "If you're quite finished rubbing yourself on Jacinth, we'll go our way and let you sink back into your no doubt well-deserved anonymity."

Harold stared at him, uncertain whether to be amused or angry. He decided to take a middle course.

"You're a hard-mouthed little bastard, aren't you?" he said. "Or so I'd be likely to think if it weren't for the reputation you Esmeraldans have for courtesy. So I guess what you were saying to me is humor. If anyone said that stuff to me seriously, I'd just be forced to beat on him until he changed his tune."

Harold grinned amicably as he said this, but spoiled the effect by losing his balance and falling against a waiter, who spilled a tray of drinks. Louvaine caught his arm and helped Harold to his feet.

"Very nice to have met you," Louvaine said. "All in fun, eh? But you must watch that lurch. Come along, Jacinth."

Jacinth blew Harold a kiss and went off with Louvaine. Harold scratched his head and went off to find Nora.

25 •••••

"You didn't seem to like Harold," Jacinth said. They had left the party and were now eating mussels and drinking beer—an old Esmeraldan custom—in a little restaurant down by the docks.

"Whatever gave you that impression? I like him very much. He's really quite perfect."

"For what?" Jacinth asked.

"Well, he'd make a great Victim. That clumsiness of his, it's really very endearing."

Jacinth thought about it. "He did seem a little . . . naive. He's just passed the Trials and signed up for the Hunt. Did you know that?"

"Interesting," Louvaine said. "He'd really make a superb target, wouldn't he? I'm signing up for the Hunt again, by the way."

"So soon after the last."

"I didn't make a very brilliant showing last time out. I need to show people once and for all that I still have all my moves."

"Wouldn't it be funny if the computer put you and Harold together?"

"Yes, very. A consummation devoutly to be wished for."

"Unlikely, though."

Louvaine nodded, and they went on to talk about other things. But he was thinking. He was dazzled by the splendor of his vision: hunting Harold, a target large enough and tall enough—for Louvaine had a tendency to fire high—for anyone to hit.

26 • • • • •

Early the next morning, Louvaine took his car and went out looking for his Uncle Ezra. He was driving his town car, a Buick Triceratops with bullet-proof glass, punctureproof tires, a superpadded interior of monocoque construction in case of collision, and oxygen equipment in the event of gas attack. Vehicles in Esmeralda tended to be functional. It was powered by a 30-liter double-camshaft 2,000-horsepower V-24 engine. A lot of power was necessary to haul the Buick's inch-thick steel plating.

All that armor played hell with performance and gas mileage, of course, but it was necessary in a place like Huntworld. There was always some oddball around who found it an irresistible prank to roll a hand grenade under a moving vehicle.

And there was another reason for armor plating: people in Esmeralda tended to drive quickly, recklessly, and without skill. Consequently there were many collisions, but no insurance, since Huntworld and its institutions had been declared uninsurable by no less a source than Lloyd's of London.

And finally there was the terrifying prospect of being hit by a motorist discharging his Reckless Driving Obligation.

Louvaine drove into the eternally slow-moving traffic jam that characterized the downtown streets near the Hunt Ministry. His Buick's dagger-shaped front end enabled him to push and squeeze between slower and more clumsily shaped vehicles. This was accompanied by a nerve-shattering screech of metal on metal which his soundproofed interior mostly shut out.

He triple-parked at a fire hydrant in a safety zone and ran up the broad marble steps of the Hunt Ministry, scattering the pigeons and squashing a little girl's peanut-butter-and-jelly sandwich in his haste.

A clerk informed him that his Uncle Ezra was not there. He was probably over at the Coliseum, supervising the preparations for the Saturnalia fights.

Louvaine got back in his car and sped to the Coliseum. On his way, more by accident than design, he clipped a cripple in a gas-powered wheelchair when the guy's supercharger failed to kick in at the last moment. That gave Louvaine a hundred points toward Driver of the Year, and even though he was in a tearing haste to see Uncle Ezra, he stopped and waited until a Traffic Checker came along and verified the kill.

Then he drove on. The incident, trifling in itself, had raised his spirits. Yes, perhaps things were going to turn his way again at last. If only Uncle Ezra could be persuaded to do one simple little thing for him.

27 • • • • •

Louvaine parked at the eastern gate of the Coliseum and hurried inside. The giant amphitheater was modeled closely on the original Colosseum in Rome. He went through the outer wall, four stories high, with its arcaded Corinthian columns, then through the second wall and onto the arena floor.

The seats sloped upward and backward on all sides. Attendants were at work attaching the awnings that would shelter the spectators from Esmeralda's fierce afternoon sun. On the arena floor the scene was one of confusion. Lighting men, sound men, cameramen, performers, agents all mingled together on the arena floor in a mess of black electrical cables and half-finished props. The scene was made all the more confusing by the presence of many delivery boys bringing in sandwiches and drinks.

Louvaine saw his Uncle Ezra across the arena. Ezra was a diminutive man with a tuft of white hair above each ear. He was rosy-cheeked and rosy-skulled, with a small pug nose and impressive eyebrows. He was sitting in front of a table filled with blueprints and plans weighted down by a brace of revolvers.

Uncle Ezra was one of the Huntworld Elders. He had reached this position by making a great deal of money trading in commercial intangibles in London and Paris and then retiring to Huntworld with his profits. He was one of the men who made Huntworld policy. Now he was working furiously on final preparations for the Big Payoff. It would be held at the end of the week, and it would mark the start of the Saturnalia season.

Saturnalia was the most important holiday in the Esmeraldan year. Like Mardis Gras or Carnival in other places, Saturnalia featured a great lot of singing in the streets and public intoxication. There would be fanciful floats with pretty half-naked girls in scanty costumes throwing flowers. Food vendors would serve specialties unobtainable the rest of the year because they were forbidden except during Saturnalia, thus helping make it a really special holiday.

A part of Uncle Ezra's work as an Elder was the mounting and staging of the various events to take place in the arena—the duels, melees, massacres, and fights to the death, and, of course, the popular Suicide Clowns.

In one way at least the Esmeraldan Games were superior to the ancient Roman gladiatorial events—previously the standard in vulgar and senseless slaughter. The old Romans didn't have the internal combustion engine and therefore were unable to stage really satisfying vehicle combats. (Although it's true that a four-chariot pileup at high speed is an event worth going out of your way to see.)

Unlike the Roman Games, the Esmeraldan Games had no animal fights. Nobody wanted to see animals killed. There were too few big animals around, even counting those in zoos. What everyone wanted to see killed was human beings—those big-brained mammals who had brought the world to its present state.

Every year the events of the arena had to be similar to what had gone before, but a little bit different so that the planners could not be accused of lack of originality. Ezra spent a lot of his time consulting with death decorators, crash consultants, pop death concept salesmen, and the like.

The climax to it all would be the Big Payoff. One

pair of Hunters, selected from all the Hunts going on in Esmeralda at the time, would finish their combat in the Coliseum in front of the sell-out crowd. It would be the main event of the Games, and no one knew in advance what weapons or conditions would be chosen.

Louvaine had always wanted to be in a Big Payoff. Win or lose, it was the shortest way to immortality. But Uncle Ezra didn't have anything to do with the selections for that. The Big Payoff was always staged by *The Huntworld Show*, and featured a Hunt picked by Gordon Philakis, the well-liked master of ceremonies.

"Uncle Ezra, how good to see you!" Louvaine said.

"Ah, Louvaine, good to see you, too. I caught the video clip of your latest kill last night on *The Late Night Hunt News*. Very amusing, I must say."

"I didn't find it so," Louvaine said.

"I suppose not. But you must admit it *was* funny, your Victim falling over a garbage can and breaking his neck while you broke all the windows in the neighborhood."

"Look, can't we talk about something else?"

"Of course, my boy. What would you like to talk about?"

"I'm signing up for another Hunt," Louvaine said.

"Excellent idea. But don't you think you might want to take a course first in Remedial Shooting?"

"There's nothing wrong with my aim," Louvaine said. "I'm just having bad luck."

"We all get that from time to time," Ezra said. "It'll pass."

"I plan to make it pass," Louvaine said.

"Excellent attitude."

"I'll need your help, though."

Ezra looked at him sternly. "If it's a matter of arranging somebody's death, I told you last time I would never do that again."

"That's not the favor I need," Louvaine said. "I'm perfectly capable of killing my own people, thank you very much."

"Then what's the problem?"

"Perhaps you'll agree," Louvaine said, "that in order to have a good fight one needs a good opponent. That's what they used to say in the days of the old Spanish bullfight."

"That makes sense, I'm sure," Ezra said. "But what has that got to do with me? If you expect me to arrange a fight for you with a bull—"

"No, you're getting it all mixed up," Louvaine said. "What I want you to do is very simple. There is a fellow in town named Harold Erdman. He has just signed up for his first Hunt."

"Nothing unusual about that. People do it all the time."

"I want you to arrange for the computer to pick me as his Victim."

"But that's against the rules."

"Of course it's against the rules," Louvaine said testily. "That's why I'm asking you to arrange it for me."

"My dear boy, I have a reputation for honesty in this town."

"It isn't as if we're going to tell anyone," Louvaine pointed out "And even if it is against the rules, it's not against the *spirit* of the rules."

"How do you differentiate?"

"The spirit of the rules is to produce good fights. If you can set me up with this one, I can guarantee it'll be an absolute peak experience."

"What's the matter with the fellow?" Ezra asked. "Got a broken leg or something?"

"No, no, he's perfectly sound. But he's a novice. Sort of slow and clumsy, and a bit stupid, too, I think."

"I'll say this for you," Ezra said. "You can really pick them. He does sound like a perfect victim."

"And, of course, him not knowing that I know he's hunting me would be of some help, too."

"It would give you quite an advantage," Ezra said.

"Sure, it's an advantage," Louvaine said. "But I'm doing it for the sake of show business and to save our family name from people laughing at it when they watch the video clips."

"I don't like to bend the rules," Ezra said, "but it's true, we can't have people laughing at us, even if your last Hunt *was* laughable."

"Will you do this for me, Uncle?"

His uncle winked at him. "We'll see. And now, scat. I'm busy."

28 • • • • •

Several days later, Harold went for a walk down to the open-air market near the port, where the old town hall had stood. It was a picturesque place filled with stalls piled high with clothing, foodstuffs, and flowers under a corrugated iron roof painted with pink and white stripes. Here were displayed goods from all over the earth, and even a few imported specialties from Mars Colony.

Harold was feeling pretty good. With the money left over from the bonus he had bought himself some new clothes and extra cartridges for the Smith & Wesson, and had rented a small furnished apartment in the Old Quarter, not far from where Nora lived.

He came by the flower stands and saw the girl he had met at the Jubilee Ball. Jacinth, that was her name. She looked stunning in a simple white dress, an exotic creature unlike any he had known with her stylishly cut black hair and provocative crimson lips.

Jacinth asked him if he was happy in Huntworld.

Harold nodded. "This is the best I've ever had it in my life."

"You must be from one of those deprived backgrounds," Jacinth said. "I'd hate to have to live that way. Thank God my family is rich."

Jacinth's father owned a nationwide chain of butcher shops. Real meat was in constant demand and limited supply in America, and brought astronomical prices. Jacinth never had to bother her pretty

head about how to afford to travel first-class all of
the time when she wasn't in college. She was glad of
that, because if she had to worry about money she
was sure it would make her sulky and spoil her
looks.

Harold and Jacinth had lunch at one of the charm-
ing little sidewalk cafés near the market, and then
Harold offered to show her his new apartment. It
was a one-room efficiency with the usual steel shut-
tering and built-in alarm systems. When they got
there Harold found a letter in his mailbox. It had
the Huntworld seal of crossed revolvers on a field of
swords.

"It's your notification of Hunt!" Jacinth said. "Oh,
how exciting!"

Harold's first Hunt had now officially begun. He
opened the envelope. His first Victim was a man
named Louvaine Daubray.

Jacinth read the name, and her big green eyes
opened wider. "Louvaine? You're fighting Louvaine!"

"That *is* a coincidence," Harold said. "He's one of
the few people that I know here. Now I'm going to
have to kill him. But of course, he and I didn't hit it
off too well anyhow."

Jacinth was thoughtful, and she left soon after that.
It bothered her that out of all the possible combinations of Hunters in Huntworld, the Hunts computer
should pick Louvaine for Harold's first Victim. She'd
heard that at any one time there were twenty-five
thousand, or perhaps it was two hundred and fifty
thousand, possible combinations of Hunters and Hunt-
eds. When she took arithmetic next year she would
have to figure out the odds against this particular
meeting.

29 • • • • •

The doorbell chimed. Teresa went to answer it. "Someone to see you," she called to Albani.

"Who is it?" Albani asked.

"Says his name's Harold."

Albani had been reclined on the chaise longe, passing a dreamy afternoon with the *Comic Book Encyclopedia of the World*. He liked to combine education and entertainment. He bounded to his feet now, pulled his pale brown water-figured silk dressing gown more tightly around him, squared his shoulders, turned on his smile, and went to the door.

"Harold! How good to see you. Come right in!" He gave Teresa the nod which meant go fetch the wine and poppy cakes, and led Harold to the sunroom. "Been enjoying yourself here?"

"No complaints so far," Harold said in his pleasant slow voice.

"Let's just hope it goes on that way," Albani said, superstitiously crossing his fingers and eyes. "Here, sit down, take the comfortable chair. You're really lucky to be here at this time of year. Saturnalia season is always such fun. A man would have to go a long way to find a better place to die than Huntworld during Saturnalia. Not that I mean you're *going* to die, I just mean if it *should* happen. Have you gotten your Hunt notification yet?"

Harold nodded and took the slip of paper out of his pocket. Albani read it. A frown crossed his handsome features. "Louvaine? You're fighting Louvaine Daubray? How very extraordinary!"

"Why's that?"

"It's just unusual for someone who's only been here a few days to have the computer pick one of the few people he knows for his first Hunt."

"Jacinth thought so too," Harold said. "But what the hell, there it is. He signed up to kill or be killed, same as me. I won't let the fact that I don't like him stand in the way of my killing him. Frankly, I'd like to do it and get it over with as soon as possible. That's why I've come to you, Mike. I want you to be my Spotter."

Teresa came back with the wine and poppy cakes. Albani said, "Harold here wants me to Spot for him."

"He couldn't have picked a better man," Teresa said loyally.

"It's true, even if I do say so myself," Albani said. "He's fighting Louvaine," he told Teresa.

"I've heard about that one," Teresa said. "Sloppy killer, isn't he?"

"Very sloppy," Albani said. "His most recent Hunt ended with his victim dying accidentally of a broken neck. You can't get much sloppier than that."

"I'm new at this stuff," Harold said. "But one thing I can tell you: I'm not sloppy."

"The question is," Albani said, "are you lucky? Louvaine is sloppy but lucky. So far it's proved an unbeatable combination."

Harold shrugged. "I think I'm lucky, too."

"We'll see," Albani said. He gave Teresa a look. Discreetly she left the room. The two men sipped the wine and nibbled the poppy cakes. Then Albani said, "I've got a pretty busy schedule, what with Saturnalia coming up and all. But yes, I think I can accommodate you."

"Glad to hear that," Harold said. "I figure you and I are going to make a good combination."

"If only you could know how much I hope that's true," Albani said. "Well, first things first. There's the matter of my fee."

"That's the only problem," Harold said.

"How can that be a problem? You've just gotten your bonus, haven't you?"

"Yes, but I've already spent it," Harold said, "and I won't get any more until I make my kill."

"Damnation," Albani said. "This is no way to do business, though it's typical enough."

"You'll get the whole thing, plus a nice bonus on top of the bonus, as soon as I put down Louvaine."

"That's decent of you," Albani said. "But you mean 'if,' not 'when.'"

"I figure, with a man like you Spotting for me, it's pretty much a sure thing," Harold said.

Albani knew when he was being flattered. He liked it. What he didn't like was working without being paid first. But he needed the job. If Harold made a good kill it would help him a lot with his difficulties.

"Well," he said, "since you give me no choice, I accept."

"I'd hoped you would," Harold said.

Albani shook his hand, then called for Teresa. "Take away his wine," he told her. "Give him a glass of water. You are in strict training now. We'll choose some weapons for you, then go out to the practice range."

"Can't I just go out and find Louvaine and get it over with?"

"Soon," Albani said. "But I like your spirit."

30 • • • • •

Albani took Harold down to the training and practice center which the government of Esmeralda maintained free of charge for all Hunters and Victims. There were facilities for sports like basketball and volleyball, a swimming pool, and the usual array of exercising machinery. They walked past dueling strips where men fenced with saber and foil. Some were fighting with slim daggers. Others worked out with various other kinds of bludgeons, clubs, axes, and similar instruments. In another section there were baths and massage rooms.

"The gun rooms are over here," Albani said.

"I don't want to seem naive," Harold said, "but why are all those people practicing hand-to-hand combat? Is it for sport, or physical fitness? I can't imagine that stuff would be much good against a gun."

"That's where you'd be wrong," Albani said. "Some of our most famous Hunters never carry a gun. They hunt with bare hands, or with a knife."

"Against a man with a gun?"

"Guns have their limitations," Albani said. "If you don't take your man out with the first shot, you could be in trouble. A wounded opponent is apt to be very dangerous, especially if he's on Berserkium."

"What's that?" Harold asked.

"Berserkium is one of our special-purpose drugs. A lot of people take it before going out on a Hunt. You don't even feel it unless you're wounded or under great stress. Shock triggers it off, giving you an adrenaline supercharge. While Berserkium is active in your bloodstream you can create an unbelievable amount of destruction. It only lasts a few minutes and you're completely wiped out afterward."

"Does Louvaine know this hand-to-hand stuff?" Harold asked.

"He holds various degrees in kung fu, knife fighting, club fighting, sword fighting, and one or two other kinds of fighting. I think he's done a bit of combat instructing, too."

"That's great," Harold said.

Albani was carrying a small brown leather suitcase with brass reinforcers at the corners. "This is for you to use," he said, "but after the fight I want it back." He opened the case. Inside, nested in red satin, was an SSK .45-70 with a fourteen-inch barrel.

"Take it in your hand," Albani said. "Feel the balance."

The heavy gun sat easily in Harold's big fist. It was a deadly piece of precision machinery, with its blued-steel surfaces and its polished walnut insets. Harold lifted it and admired it, then put it down.

"It's a right handsome thing," Harold said. "But I'm sticking with my Smith & Wesson."

Albani looked doubtful. "I don't mean to disparage the gun. But I can see at a glance that it's old and probably hasn't been properly maintained. What if the firing pin breaks? It's really better you go with the SSK."

"I don't want to be stubborn," Harold said, "but since I'm the one going to be pulling the trigger, I figure I get to choose what sort of a gun I pull it on."

"I can't argue with that," Albani said. "Let's see how you do on the firing range."

In the gun room, Harold practiced dry firing first

until he could do it smoothly enough to satisfy Albani. Then he and Albani went to the firing range. Harold proved to have a pretty good natural eye and a steady hand. His first shots were wide of target, but he steadied down quickly.

"Your reactions are second to none," Albani said. "You're really not bad at all."

"What does Louvaine shoot like?" Harold asked.

"Ah, well, when he's in form he's a very fine marksman. As you could be with a few months' or even weeks' work."

"But I won't have that long, will I?"

"You've got no time at all. Let's talk with a friend of mine and get his advice."

He led Harold to a little office on one side of the gym. Within, a very small, very old Chinese man, with a thin, wispy mustache, and a hat with the brim turned up all around, giving him a resemblance to Charlie Chan in the old movies, was watching the gun-room action on a tiny TV screen.

"Mr. Chang, this is my good friend and client Harold Erdman."

"Very pleased to meet you," Chang said, in a strong English accent. "I have watched your protégé's progress on my TV."

"Mr. Chang is a specialist's specialist in murder and survival. If anyone can help you, he can."

"Let me be alone with Mr. Erdman," Chang said. Albani bowed and left the office. When they were alone, Chang offered Harold a seat and poured him tea in a delicate porcelain cup. "What do you think of your chances?" Chang asked.

"I'll be all right," Harold said.

"What makes you think so?"

"I don't know," Harold said. "I just do."

"Suppose I tell you to get out quick while you're still alive?"

"I'd tell you to tell that to my Victim."

"You like the intensity of the situation," Chang suggested.

Harold nodded. "Yes, I do. I'm a little nervous about it, but I'll be all right when the time comes."

"There's no time to train you in any of the martial arts," Chang said. "There's only time to teach you one thing. Listen carefully now. In moments of danger, advantage can be gained by doing the unexpected."

"I think I've heard that before," Harold said.

"The deepest truths are always obvious. It's not what you know, it's what you can use when the time comes that counts. This Louvaine is your Victim?"

Harold nodded.

"Then I suggest you get him as soon as possible." He turned to the door. "Albani!"

Mike Albani came back inside. "Yes, Mr. Chang?"

"This boy is clumsy but he's cool. The sooner he gets this first fight behind him, the better. Don't toy with the Victim. Go out and get him as soon as possible. Now I have said enough. Good luck."

They left. Albani was thoughtful as they packed up their equipment and left the gym.

"What next?" Harold asked.

"Next I find out where Louvaine is. And then you get him."

"As simple as that?"

"I sure to God hope so."

31 • • • • •

"So how did he do, this new client of yours?" Teresa asked when Albani returned from the training center. She made it a point always to ask her husband about business when he came home at night, so that he could boast a little and not feel so stupid about the botch he was making of both their lives. Her mother had taught her this as part of the Old Wisdom.

"He concentrates well," Albani said. "And he's very determined."

"But how does he shoot?"

Albani began to look a little uncomfortable. "He's got a good eye and he doesn't flinch when he squeezes the trigger. But he hasn't had much practice. In six months he could be the best shot in this city."

"Has he a quick draw?"

"No, not yet. But given a little time—"

"Mike," Teresa said, growing faintly alarmed, "he doesn't *have* any time. He's fighting a duel right *now*."

Albani nodded and walked to the refrigerator and got himself a beer. He came back to the living room humming. Now Teresa knew there was something wrong, something he wasn't telling her.

She put down the stocking cap she had been knitting and said, "You've got yourself another loser for a client. That's it, isn't it, Michelangelo?"

"That's not it at all. Teresa, this boy's a natural."

"What does that mean?"

"Everybody's born to do something," Albani said.

"There are born painters and born auto mechanics. Born woodworkers and born swimmers. There are born Spotters, like me. That's what I mean when I say he's a natural."

"A natural Hunter?"

"Better than that. Teresa, I'm pretty sure Harold is a natural-born killer."

Teresa looked puzzled. "But aren't all Hunters killers?"

"All Hunters *kill*, sure. But that doesn't make them *killers*. Not *real* killers. A lot of them are like children, just playing a game, even though the bullets are real. Bang, bang, you're dead. But Harold ... well, Harold isn't playing at all. Harold is a serious-minded young killer and he's going to go far. I'm not the only one who thinks so. Chang watched him work out. he saw the potential."

"Well, I'm glad to hear he has a chance, you being his Spotter and all."

"Everyone but Chang and me thinks Harold's just a clown."

"I can imagine," Teresa said.

"The bookies are offering twenty to one against him. Have you ever heard such incredible odds?"

Teresa looked alert. Something bad was coming, she could just tell.

"The odds were so good," Albani said, "and what with Chang feeling the same way and all, I put down a bet on Harold."

Teresa stood up, the stocking cap falling to the floor. "A bet? But Mike, we don't have any money. Don't tell me the bookies have started giving credit!"

Albani's face was a study in discomfiture. "No, of couse not. What I did, I took out a mortgage on the house."

"Mike, you didn't! It's all we've got!"

"Look, what kind of a Spotter am I if I don't bet

on my own man? And anyhow, I had to fulfill my Gambling Obligation, or risk being in violation of the Financial Imprudence Act."

"Mike, you shouldn't have bet the house. If Harold loses it'll mean slavery for us both. You know the government doesn't tolerate people sleeping in the streets."

"But Harold's going to win. I'm sure of it. I've never been surer of anything. That's why I threw my final chip into the pot. So to speak."

"Mike, you'd better tell me what you did."

Albani heaved an explosive sigh. "The fact is, Teresa, I bet another ten thousand with Fat Freddy the bookie by giving him a chattel mortage on you. He'll never collect it, of course. Harold—"

Teresa stood up. "Am I hearing straight? Did you actually mortgage *me* in order to put a bet on that clumsy oaf bumpkin client of yours?"

"Yes, that's what I did," Albani said. "If Harold doesn't win, I'll be enslaved and probably put to work in the pigshit factory. But you'll be Fat Freddy's new chattel, which is not so bad, given the choices available. Never say I don't look out for you."

"Oh, Albani," Teresa wailed.

"Don't worry, he's going to win."

Teresa got hold of herself. She had decided in a flash what to do. She would spare Albani the indignity of laboring in the pigshit factory by killing him if Harold lost the bet. As for her, Fat Freddy was not so bad-looking if you ignored his face. And he had the reputation of being a good provider.

"Well," she said, "you know best. I just hope it works out."

"It's practically in the bag," Albani said. Not for the first time he congratulated himself on having been smart enough to pick an understanding wife. Any other woman would have scolded him for offering her up as a bet on an unknown and untested Hunter. Not Teresa.

Teresa went to the kitchen to get dinner—Beefoids in spicy Pseudomato sauce, Albani's favorite. How strange, she thought, that soon she might be cooking for Fat Freddy. According to one of her girlfriends, Fat Freddy hated Beefoids in any form. He was known to favor Mock Veal Roasters or Super Simul-Pork Roast. If Harold lost, she might never cook Beefoids again. Life was strange.

32 •••••

Nora was sitting in the window seat in her apartment, legs tucked under her, looking out the window. She looked real pretty with the light outlining her clear features and catching highlights from her crisp blond hair.

"Harold," she said after a while, "what was the name of that commune?"

"What commune?"

"The one you told me about. The one the Catskill Kid was going to."

"Oh. La Hispanidad, I think he said it was. Over to Lake Okeechobee, that's where he said it was."

"Did it sound nice?"

"It sounded all right, the way he told it. Why?"

"Do you think you could ever live in a place like that?"

Harold laughed. "Commune's just a fancy word for a farm. I've seen enough of those."

"But this would be different. This'd be a place where everybody would be working together, sharing."

"And singing songs in Spanish? Hell, Nora, any way you cut it, it's still farm work."

"And you're finished with farming?"

"So far I like it here just fine. City life's not so hard to take. You planning on going to a Spanish commune in Florida, Nora?"

She shook her head and came out of the window-seat. "I was just having a little fantasy. I like it fine here in Esmeralda. Especially now that you've come here."

"That's nice of you, Nora," Harold said.

33 ● ● ● ● ●

Jacinth had lunch with Uncle Ezra at the Hunt Club's private dining room. They ate real food, not the synthetic stuff that the sustenance factories of the world kept churning out. Jacinth didn't really like real food—at school she lived on Zeroburgers, with no calories or carbohydrates. But she knew real food was expensive, so she was determined to learn to like it. They taught her in school that a taste for anything expensive can be acquired, if one is willing to work hard enough at it.

They were on the roof terrace of Esmeralda's tallest building, only twenty-two stories but commanding a splendid panoramic view of the entire island.

On the wall behind them, a gigantic monitor was tuned to *The Huntworld Show*. It flashed pictures of bloody street corners filled with curious crowds staring at draped forms lying on the ground in puddles of blood that sometimes came through a bright green due to atmospheric conditions which affected the automatic color-matching monitor. A voice-over commented, "Hi, this is Gordon Philakis, bringing you a summary of the day's Hunting events. Early this afternoon Luther Fabius from Berlinsberg, West Germany, scored a clean kill over Biff Edmonson, of Calgary, Canada. If any of Biff's friends or kinfolk are listening, I want you to know he died a quick death doing what he wanted to do. Al McTaggart, the three-Hunt victor from Boise, Idaho, tagged out Hernán Ibañez, the five-Hunt switch shooter from

Buenos Aires. And this just in: Al Smith of Lansing, Michigan, just put down Edvard Grieg, of Oahu, Hawaii, but was fined ten points when his submachine gun went out of control and wounded several people in the crowd. You'll never get to be Hunter of the Year that way, Ed. . . .

"And now on a lighter note, Maxwell Santini, a waiter at the Surfeater Arms in downtown Esmeralda, was killed this afternoon when he went to the room of Mr. V. S. Mikkleston, of London, England, carrying a ham and swiss on rye on a tray, and was impaled in the chest by a throwing knife when he opened the door. Mikkleston claimed that Santini didn't knock, just 'walked in without warning and fell foul to a spot of target practice with the old stiletto.' Santini's union claimed personal malice—the sandwich had been over an hour late—and took the matter to court. The ruling, rendered this afternoon, exonerated the Hunter, stating, "What does a waiter more or less matter, anyway?"

Jacinth raised her hand, causing the newscast screen to contract into a glowing pip, shielding them both from the light and sound of *The Huntworld Show*.

"All that sweetness and light makes me cross," she said. "Louvaine always has it on, too."

"Eh?" said Uncle Ezra, making use of the expletive which on Esmeralda is reserved for older people. "Doing all right, is he?"

"I suppose so—nothing's happened yet. Funny the computer should match those two. The selection is supposed to be random, isn't it?"

Ezra smiled and winked.

"Uncle, did you have anything to do with getting those two into a duel together?"

"I didn't do a thing," Ezra said. "I just asked the Hunt computer to do me a little favor. It knows which side its circuits are buttered on, so to speak."

"I thought computers weren't supposed to be able to do things like that."

"They will if they're fitted with the new Operator Preference Override Superimposing Code-Writing Program."

"You cheated in order for Louvaine and Harold to meet! You evil old man!"

Ezra beamed. He loved to hear pretty young girls call him an evil old man.

"Yes, at Louvaine's request I set it up. The boy needs an easy kill, Jacinth. Something to restore his confidence. He used to be good, Jacinth, very, very good. Louvaine was the classiest killer this town had seen in a long time. And he can be good again, with a little help."

"But what you did was cheating," Jacinth asked.

Ezra shrugged. "What does a little cheating matter when it's for the family?"

Jacinth returned to Louvaine's apartment thinking rather more deeply than she was accustomed to do. She found herself, in fact, in a dilemma. She wasn't really certain that cheating, even for family, was right. Especially when this cheating was going to result in the death of Harold, a young man she had found not too unattractive and whom she was planning on dating as soon as she found a way to get him to ask her.

The more she thought about it, the more wrong cheating seemed, though she couldn't put her finger on why. And the question really was, what should *she* do? It was really uncomfortable now knowing. She considered flipping a coin, then finally tabled the question by popping a sleeping pill.

34 • • • • •

Harold had just settled down for a nap in his new apartment when the telephone rang. It was Albani.

"Harold? I need you right away."

"What's happening?"

"Something important. Get over here quick. Don't forget your gun." He hung up.

Harold had been fully dressed. All he had to do was slip on his sneakers and check the load in the Smith & Wesson. Albani had insisted earlier that a gunsmith look it over. The gunsmith had replaced the barrel and all moving parts. Harold had test-fired it and had to admit it aimed better. But it still had the old feel, and that was important.

When he got to Albani's house, Teresa showed him to the basement. Albani had his office there. There were maps on every wall, showing Esmeralda and the rest of the island in great detail. A ham radio sat on one table with a multiphone switchboard beside it. There was a small bronze replica of Rodin's *Thinker* on Albani's worktable. It was the famous Deathmaster Award for Best Spotter of the Year. But it was five years old, won when the fabulous Sanchez was still alive.

Albani was munching one of Teresa's miniature pizzas and talking to somebody on the telephone. He waved Harold to take a seat. Harold pushed aside a stack of back-issue *ManKiller* magazines and sat down.

"Yeah," Albani was saying. "Yeah, I hear you. . . Yeah. . . . Yeah. . . ."

Teresa said to Harold, "Would you like a miniature pizza?"

"Yes, ma'am, I would."

"I have one kind with anchovy and another kind with pepperoni. Which would you like?"

"You pick for me," Harold said, clearly meaning both. Teresa gave him two of each and a glass of beer.

"No beer for him," Albani said. "He's in training." Then back to the phone. "Yeah. . . . Yeah. . . ."

"These are really good," Harold said.

"It's my mother's recipe," Teresa said. "From Sicily."

"All right," Albani said into the phone. "We're moving. I'll contact you next on channel 5 on the CB radio."

He hung up and said to Harold, "I think we've got him."

"Louvaine?"

"Who else would I be talking about, Zasu Pitts? Yes, Louvaine, big as life and twice as snotty. He's just gone into a bar downtown in the Latin Quarter, a place called La Petite Moue, and ordered a double frozen strawberry daiquiri. He's out there in the open, and we're going to get to nail that sucker right now."

"You mean right *now*?"

"I sure as hell don't mean next Thursday. You got your gun? Is it loaded? Let me see."

"*Come on*," Harold said.

"I'm your Spotter, I have to check the details." He looked at Harold's gun and handed it back. "OK, let's move."

"How come he's just sitting there like that?" Harold asked. "Do you think he didn't get his Hunt notification yet?"

"That would be too much to hope for. But it has been known to happen."

"It doesn't seem fair to kill him if he doesn't even know he's being Hunted."

"It's perfectly fair," Albani said. "I'll explain it to you later." He took a high-powered hunting rifle with an infrared sniperscope off the wall, checked its load, and stuck it into a gun bag.

"What's that for?" Harold asked.

"Just in case God, in His infinite mercy, grants us a nice clean shot from beyond pistol range."

"Michelangelo," Teresa said, "you shouldn't blaspheme."

"Who's blaspheming? I'm praying. Let's go, Harold. He won't sit there forever even if he is working on a double frozen strawberry daiquiri."

The Café La Petite Moue had a glassed-in front which extended over the sidewalk. Albani, with Harold beside him, was examining it from the shadowed entrance of a bar across the street with high-powered binoculars.

"It's him," Albani said. "Look for yourself."

Harold took the glasses and saw Louvaine's long-nosed profile bent over a very large violently colored drink.

Harold said, "I guess you were pretty smart, bringing along that rifle. I could get him right through the window."

"Forget it," Albani said. "Bulletproof. But look to your left. The side door of the café is open. You'll go around the block and approach from the other side. That'll put you behind him. As you come past that mailbox there you'll have a clear shot through the open door into the café. You'll have to keep your gun hidden until the last moment. We don't want spectators reacting and giving away the show. You got it?"

"Yes, I got it," Harold said.

"Then go out and do it," Albani said.

Harold stood perfectly still for a moment, and Albani wondered if he was going to freeze up on him. That's all he needed, a first-time Hunter with stage fright. He really should have insisted on payment in advance.

Then Harold gave him a quick nod and slid out the door. Albani watched him go, and something like an emotion arose in his chest. This boy was going to be all right.

Louvaine wondered why on earth he had ordered a double frozen strawberry daiquiri. Probably because it was big enough and colorful enough for even so dull-witted a Spotter as Albani and his associates to discover. He took a sip. Too sweet, as usual. Then he winced as the tiny radio receiver in his ear crackled with static. It was Souzer, reporting from the rooftop.

"They've arrived," Souzer said. "Albani and Erdman. They're in the entrance of the bar across the street. They're looking over the setup."

"I wish they'd hurry," Louvaine said, subvocalizing into the tiny throat microphone. "This drink is giving me a headache."

"Harold's coming out now," Souzer said. "He's going around the block, just like I figured he would. Are you ready?"

Louvaine nodded, then realized that Souzer couldn't see him through five floors of concrete and steel. "Yes, I'm ready."

"Is the mirror OK?"

"Yes, it's working fine."

Previously prepared by Souzer and set above him on the café wall was a small telescopic mirror. Through it Louvaine could see the street down which Harold would come. In his hand he held the transmitter, disguised as a pack of cigarettes, which would set off the shotgun Souzer had rigged inside the mailbox. Louvaine would have to press the switch just at the moment Harold appeared in the mirror. The double blast at ten-foot range ought to take care of the rest.

It was a pretty good plan, especially on short notice, and it was nice that Albani had been dumb enough to fall for it. Louvaine only hoped nobody else was passing the mailbox when he let Harold have it. His uncle Ezra had had some difficulty fixing things a few Hunts ago when Louvaine had thrown a hand grenade at a target in a crowded department store, getting his man and a few others besides. Ironically enough, the store had been having a sale on bulletproof vests.

"He's coming around the corner now," Souzer reported. "Get ready, he's only about ten feet from the mailbox, he . . ."

"What?" Louvaine asked. "What's happening?"

"He's stopped."

"What do you mean, he's stopped? He can't stop! What's going on?"

"Somebody is talking to him. Oh my God!"

"What is it! Who's he talking to?"

"It's that goddam Gordon Philakis!"

35 • • • • •

Huntworld had seven television channels. Six of them showed reruns brought in by satellite from the United States. The seventh, devoted to round-the-clock coverage of Hunting activities, was *The Huntworld Show*, with its popular master of ceremonies, Gordon Philakis.

Philakis had a square tanned face and a big jaw and brush-cut hair. He had a breezy, rapid-fire delivery and was never at a loss for words, even when he had nothing much to say, which, considering the nature of live broadcasting, was much of the time.

"Hi, folks, this is Gorden Philakis bringing you *The Huntworld Show* straight from the capital of the killers, good old Esmeralda in the sunny Caribbean. Yes, friends, it's the friendly live local murder program with the international following. It's the program that some governments tried to ban because they thought you folks out there needed protection from the sight of real live honest-to-Sam mayhem and that you ought to be happy with the fake crime shows your own studios keep on producing. But you didn't let them do it, and I take off my hat to you. When they tried to ban us, you kept right on buying our cassettes under the counter, because you knew it's perfectly all right to watch scenes of actual violence as long as those scenes are only between consenting adults.

"Once again, ladies and gentlemen, our camera crew is roving the streets of Esmeralda, bringing you interviews with participating Hunters, zeroing in for the kills, bringing you all the thrills and chills of the wonderful world of violence.

"Excuse me, sir, I see by your badge that you are a Hunter. Is that a Smith & Wesson you're carrying?"

"Huh? Oh, yeah. If you'll excuse me—"

"How many Hunts have you had, Mr.—?"

"Erdman. Harold Erdman. This is my first."

"A first-time Hunter! How about that, folks? Where do you come from, Harold?"

"Look," Harold said, "I'd love to talk with ya some other time, but right now—"

Philakis smiled knowingly. "Whatsa matter, you got a case of Tourist Tummy, or, as some call it, the Huntworld Heaves?"

"No, nothing like that."

"Then tell us what's the trouble. We're all just plain folks around here, we'll understand, no matter what it is. Got a date with some little cutie?"

"Well, if you must know," Harold said. "I was just about to kill somebody."

"Oh, you're Hunting! You should have mentioned it in the first place! Probably a little late now. But don't worry, you'll catch up with your Victim later. You're not sore about this, are you, Harold?"

Harold grinned. "Maybe it's all for the best. I didn't have a real good feeling about this setup, you know?"

Philakis nodded solemnly. "Hunter's instinct. All the good ones have it. Who's your Spotter, Harold?"

"Mike Albani."

"Of course, one of our well-known and well-liked old-timers. He's been having a run of bad luck recently, but you'll change all that, won't you?"

"Do my best," Harold said.

"Listen, Harold," Philakis said, "I feel a little bad about you missing out on what might have been a good chance for a kill. Maybe I can make it up to you. Have you had dinner yet?"

Harold hadn't.

"Good! How would you like to be our guest reviewer on *The Huntworld Restaurant Review Show*? Come on, we're going to do it right now. You'll get one of the best dinners on the island, and we'll get a few laughs, I hope."

Philakis linked his arm with Harold's and walked him down the street, followed by camera and sound-men and the usual crowd of people hoping to get in front of the camera so they could see themselves later on the TV news.

They soon reached the restaurant, a place called Le Morganthau. Philakis, Harold, cameramen, light-ing men, script girls, assistants, and junior account executives squeezed into the vestibule, where they were greeted by good smells and a small worried-looking man in his forties wearing a white tuxedo.

"Why, hello, Gordon!" the small man said.

"Hello, Tom," Philakis said. "We decided to review your restaurant tonight."

"Oh my God," Tom said.

"We've brought along a guest reviewer. Tom, meet Mr. Harold Erdman, a recent arrival to our sunny shores, an accredited Hunter, and your guest for dinner. Harold, all you have to do is eat and give us your opinion of the food."

Tom directed Harold to a table, and the light men arranged a nice backlighting. Silverware and napkins were laid out. A red wine with a genuine French label was brought, uncorked, poured. Harold raised the glass to his lips, tasted it thoughtfully, swallowed.

"Well, Harold?" Philakis said. "What do you think?" He winked.

Harold understood. There comes a time in the life of a man when a sudden insight must help him overcome the limits of decency and fair play with which he was conditioned since childhood.

Harold was up to the occasion. He said, "Well, it's not bad— "

Philakis gave him a look that said, plain as day, "You're blowing it."

"—not bad for cleaning floors, that is."

That broke them up.

Harold disparaged course after course in words of scorn which he thought up in desperate haste beforehand in a desperate effort not to seem countrified. Some of his sallies were not bad—to call the green turtle soup a "fen of stagnant waters" was pretty good on short notice.

Philakis took some of the pressure off him by breaking in every now and then to condemn the decor, the waiters, the service, the band, the owner, the owner's wife, even the owner's cocker spaniel.

While this was going on, the *Huntworld Show* Bullies—four beefy men in two-piece swim suits carrying baseball bats—demolished the place, all except the corner where Harold was finishing the crêpes Suzette, which he characterized as sweet cold soup over a thin flapjack, just barely good enough for hogs.

To end it off, everyone gave Harold a nice round of applause when he spat out the espresso.

At last, when there was nothing left to eat or destroy, Gordon Philakis draped his arm affectionately over the owner's shoulder and told him he'd been a real good sport. The studio would of course pay for all the damage. And as a reward for being so nice about it, Gordon Philakis presented him with a box seat for the Huntworld Games.

"And thank you, too, Harold," he said, "for having been a real good sport and getting right into the spirit of things. We look forward to seeing you again soon, maybe with news of your first kill."

36 • • • • •

Albani entered his house and threw his camel's-hair coat across a chair with a violent gesture. Without looking up from the TV, Teresa asked, "So how did it go today?"

"Disaster. We had the Victim dead to rights, and then that damned Gordon Philakis and his stupid *Huntworld Show* came along and interviewed Harold. We missed a perfect setup."

"Never mind, dear, you'll kill next time."

"I hope so," Albani said. "It might not be so easy next time."

"How do you think Harold is doing."

"Pretty well. I think he has at least one good kill in him. I hope so. We really need a good one."

"Would it improve our situation?" Teresa asked wistfully.

"Frankly, it could do me a lot of good. Quite a few people are watching me on this one. There have been rumors—don't try to tell me otherwise—that I'm starting to slip."

"How dare they!" Teresa said.

"They cite the failure of my recent ambushes as an example of my failing powers of execution and judgment."

"You know," Teresa said, "they just might have a point there. There was the matter of Jeffries."

Albani winced.

"And your client before that. What was his name?"

"Antonelli. Oh, God, don't remind me." Albani

took off his jacket and loosened his tie. "Antonelli. A really generous guy. I wanted to make it extra nice for him. I had his kill all lined up. A sixteen-year-old girl, can you imagine? A virgin! That is to say, out on her first Hunt."

"Children these days will do anything," Teresa said.

"It was so simple. Antonelli had her lined up. All he had to do was squeeze the trigger. But he paused, the bloody sybarite. Had her dead in his sights and he stopped, *tasting* the kill. It's true that the girl had next to nothing on. Antonelli thought he was safe. No weapon in sight. She had counted on his response. It gave her that split second she needed in order to strangle him with her constricting hair net."

"I can't imagine how she got a permit for a weapon like that," Teresa said.

"That's not important," Albani said. "What's important is that I didn't figure it out beforehand. It's another blot on my record. Teresa, do you think I'm slipping?"

"It's not your fault," Teresa said. "What you have to do is keep your mind on business. Has he got a chance, this Harold?"

"Who knows? Who cares?" Albani said, waving his arms dramatically. "No, he doesn't stand a bloody chance in hell. But he has to win. I have to arrange it somehow. Because everything is riding on this. That's more important than someone's stupid life, isn't it?"

"My dear, I'm sure it is. But you'll think of something. Now come to dinner."

37 • • • • •

Back at his apartment, Louvaine thought long and deeply. It was really a pity he had missed this chance at getting Harold. Jacinth came in, saw him hunched over his planning table, changed her clothes, and went out again. Night came. Louvaine made himself a light dinner of poached lobster tails on toast points.

Later, Souzer came over, poured himself a drink, sat down in a chrome-and-leather sling chair, and waited for Louvaine to notice him.

Presently Louvaine stirred. He went to his writing desk, found his address book, flipped through it, came to an entry, pursed his lips, nodded.

"Souzer," he said.

"Yes, boss?"

"You know Horton Foote, don't you?"

"Sure."

"Do you know where to find him? Right now, I mean?"

"He's probably down in Clancy's Bar near the Trocadero, drinking and feeling sorry for himself."

"I want you to go out and bring him to me. Immediately."

"Sure, boss. But you know that Foote is bad news. He's also about the worst enemy you've got on this island."

"That's what makes him so perfect," Louvaine said.

"I see," Souzer said. He didn't, but there was no sense asking. The boss liked to keep his little secrets.

He started to the door. Louvaine said, "Oh, and one thing more."

Souzer paused at the door. "Yes, boss?"

"On your way down, tell the doorman to have them gas up my car. Not the Buick, the Mercedes."

Souzer wanted to ask what the plan was, but he knew better. Louvaine would tell him when he wanted to. He went out.

Louvaine spent the next hour on the phone, calling friends all over the city. He had just finished the last, an hour later, when Foote arrived.

Foote was a little man in his late thirties with a brown seamed face. He was wearing a soiled white suit, snap-brim fedora, and open-weave sandals.

"Take a seat," Louvaine said. "Help yourself to a drink. You're probably wondering why I asked you here."

"That's the only reason I came," Foote said. He helped himself to Louvaine's best bourbon.

"I know that you hate me," Louvaine said. "You think I killed your brother unfairly in a Hunt some time ago. Isn't that right?"

"Well? Didn't you?"

"Just between us," Louvaine said, "yes, I did."

Foote was caught without an immediate answer to this. He nodded and said, "Well, I thought so." He wished he could get angry.

"You weren't too fond of your brother, as I recall it," Louvaine said.

"I hated the son of a bitch and wished him dead!" Foote cried passionately. "But what has that got to do with it? I can't let people go around knocking over members of my family. How do you think it looks?"

"Well," Louvaine said, "I've asked you here now in order to make it up to you."

"And how do you propose to do that?" Foote sneered.

"Through satisfying two of your greatest loves."

"And what are they?"

"Well, one is money."

"Money," Foote said, and the sound of the word was like honey in his mouth. "Are you proposing to give me money?" His expression had brightened considerably.

"Certainly not," Louvaine said. "That would be demeaning for you."

"Yes, I suppose it would," Foote said sadly.

"What I propose is to let you work for it."

"Oh," said Foote, still disappointed.

"But you'll be working at your second-greatest love."

"Which is?"

"Treachery."

Foote leaned back in his chair. Life was not hopeless after all. There were some days when things seemed to break in your favor and good luck came from what had previously seemed the most unlikely source.

"How well you know me!" Foote said.

"You really *need* treachery, don't you?" Louvaine said. "You need it for your everyday existence. Otherwise you don't feel right."

"It's insightful of you to realize that," Foote said. "My psychiatrist says I need a steady diet of treachery in order to maintain my emotional stability. He said cold-blooded murder would be good for me, too, but I vetoed that—a man could get killed trying that sort of thing. No offense meant; to each his own."

"And none taken," Louvaine said. "I'm proposing to pay you five thousand dollars to do something you'll find quite enjoyable."

"Make it ten," Foote said, "and I'll enjoy it even more."

"We'll close at seven five," Louvaine said, "because we're old friends underneath all the hate. Eh?"

"Done," Foote said. "Who do I betray? Or is it whom?"

"One of your friends, Michelangelo Albani."

"Albani!" Foote said. "But he and I are really close. To betray him would be really bad."

"Well, so what?" Louvaine said. "That's what treachery's all about, isn't it?"

"I guess it is," Foote said. "You have a clear way of looking at things, Louvaine."

Louvaine shrugged modestly and outlined what he had in mind.

Foote nodded, then had a last-minute qualm. "This could be very bad for Albani. If he fails this time he could go into bankruptcy. You know what that means?"

"The alternative, let me point out, is that his client, Harold, kills me, thus giving Albani the bonus and the publicity he so badly needs. Would it really bother you so much if Albani went bankrupt?"

Foote considered. "Actually, with Albani sent away as a government slave, I'd have a chance of getting Teresa. Have you seen her, Louvaine? He always leaves her at home, the sly dog. She's the cutest thing—"

Louvaine cut him off with an impatient wave of a manicured hand. "I didn't ask you here to discuss dating. We are discussing money and treachery."

"Well, I'm your man. How do you want me to proceed?"

Louvaine went to the wall where his awards and prizes were displayed in glass and silver frames. He removed one, took out the paper within and gave it to Foote, then replaced the empty frame.

"You know what this is, don't you?"

"It's a Treachery Card. I've never actually held one before, but I know what it is."

"Listen carefully. Here's what I want you to do."

38 • • • • •

Early the next morning, Albani learned through his sources that Louvaine had taken his big armored Mercedes, collected a few congenial friends, and gone out to his villa in the Esmeraldan countryside to give a pre-Saturnalia party. Albani called the Spotters' Information Service and had them send over by messenger a set of plans for the villa and a map of the surrounding countryside. As he had feared, Louvaine's villa was well and thoroughly guarded.

He was considering this when the phone rang and one of his informants called in with interesting news. It seemed that one of Albani's friends, Horton Foote, had somehow acquired a Treachery Card and was willing to sell it.

A Treachery Card! That was the break Albani had been waiting for.

Albani tried to telephone Foote, but the man's service had been disconnected. Next he telephoned several of his associates. According to one, Foote had been seen hanging around the zoo, a morose figure in the long black raincoat he wore on occasions of utter dejection. Albani's informant said that Foote had given the impression of a man so depressed he would feed himself to the lions except that he dreaded the chagrin he would feel when the beasts rejected him. Another informant had seen Foote leaning against a bollard on the Southside docks, staring at the flotsam that he was no doubt contemplating becoming a part of.

*   *   *

"He sounds in pretty bad shape," Albani said to Harold over lunch. "He sounds suicidal, and that's good for us. We ought to get that card for a good price."

"I don't understand," Harold said. "What's a Treachery Card?"

"It's something the government issues from time to time on a random basis. With a Treachery Card, you can get anyone to go against his basic loyalties. It's the key to getting into Louvaine's villa without Louvaine learning about it."

"And then?" Harold asked.

"And then you blow him away, of course." He looked at his watch. "Three o'clock already? We're going to have to hurry. The party is tonight. According to my information, Louvaine will be returning to the city in the morning to get ready for Saturnalia. You have to get to his villa tonight in order to catch him by surprise. If we miss this chance, things might get awkward."

"All right," Harold said. "I'm ready."

"First we have to find Horton Foote. We'll split up. I'll see if he's still at the zoo. You look for him at the Southside docks. As soon as we have that card, we go out and finish Louvaine off."

39 • • • • •

Albani was in a foul mood as he got behind the wheel of his white Lamborghini and set off in the direction of the zoo. He was more than a little depressed. He suspected that he had done it again—bet on a loser, staked his remaining credibility on an idiot who didn't know enough to be scared and couldn't move fast enough when an opportunity presented itself.

It was true that newcomers to the Hunt often did surprisingly well against experienced Hunters. Something about Esmeralda's perennial atmosphere of risk tended to habituate longtime Hunters to the ever-present peril. They got careless.

But Louvaine, despite appearances to the contrary, was wary and ingenious. One of his early kills had been a masterpiece of its kind. Disguised as a surgeon, he had shot down his sad-eyed Latvian Victim inside the operating room at the Sisters of Mercy Hospital before the white-sheeted man could open fire with his double-barreled prosthetic. What could Harold do that would come up to that? It was probably too much to expect a really stylish kill from a hayseed. But if he got that Treachery Card he would still have a chance.

So intently had Albani been thinking about his problems that he had been driving automatically, paying only the most cursory attention to the traffic signs. He realized his mistake when a siren sounded behind him. He pulled to the curb and a police car pulled in behind him. A policeman got out. He wore a pressed khaki uniform, polished black boots, sunglasses, and a Sam Browne belt from which dangled two holstered .44 magnums.

"Going a little slow back there, weren't you?" the cop said with deceptive mildness. "Didn't you read the roadsign?"

"Yes, officer," Albani said. "It said 'Dangerous curve ahead—speed up.' And I was *going* to speed up, but my foot slipped off the pedal and the brakes locked. It could happen to anyone."

"I've been watching you," the policeman said. "You've been going ten miles under the speed limit all through the city. Whatsamatter, you trying to make fun of our reckless-driving law?"

"Certainly not! said Albani. "I'm one of the wildest drivers on this island."

The cop gave him a fishy look; he had heard it all before. He walked around Albani's car checking for violations. It was Albani's bad luck that he hadn't been maintaining his car in approved Esmeraldan fashion. Now the cop found that all his lights and blinkers were working, in open violation of the Unsafe Driving Act.

"That's it," the cop said. "I'm issuing you with a Reckless Driving Obligation."

Albani pleaded in vain as the cop fitted the special equipment to his car's computerized operating panel. He begged for a postponement, even offered a sizable bribe. But it was his bad luck to have gotten his summons on a Bribeless Tuesday.

When the equipment was in place the cop looked at him through the car window, making sure his seat belt was not in place.

"Good luck, buddy," he said. "It's only a ten-minute fine and traffic's not too heavy today."

The cop moved out of the way as the special equipment took over, slamming down Albani's accelerator. The car took off in a screech and stink of burning rubber.

Word of a Reckless Driving Obligation gets around fast. Cars, trucks, and buses ran themselves up onto the sidewalks. Pedestrians ducked into doorways and into car-raid shelters as Albani hurtled down the thoroughfare in his hot Lamborghini.

He managed to hang a screaming left turn onto the main highway out of the city. Acceleration pressed him back in his seat as he cut in and out of traffic. The wobble command kicked in, sending him fishtailing across the highway, into a field, and back onto a secondary road. Albani wrestled the steering wheel like a man trying to subdue a python, stabbing intermittently at the brakes, trying not to burn them out.

The climax came when he saw, a hundred yards ahead of him, a traffic jam snarling up all the available roadway. Albani threw the car into a four-wheel drift and closed his eyes.

At that moment his Obligation elapsed and the accelerator pedal popped up. Quickly Albani pressed the parachute release, an emergency measure with which all cars in Esmeralda were equipped. He slewed to a stop a few feet from a crowded traffic intersection.

He was able then to proceed to the zoo at a sedate pace. As a reward for having survived the Reckless Driving Obligation, drivers were granted twenty four hours of the most outlandish safety driving they cared to attempt. In Albani's case, it was twenty miles an hour all the way.

At the zoo an attendant thought for a long time and then, upon receipt of a crisp five-dollar bill, remembered a man who looked just like Horton Foote and had spent a long time watching the baboons. The guy had left half an hour ago.

40 • • • • •

Albani rushed back to the city, breaking enough safety regulations to satisfy the most exigent of policemen. Harold meanwhile had proceeded to the waterfront. Foote was reputed to hang out in a place called Mulligan's Last Chance Saloon & Flophouse. It was a tall, narrow structure near the docks.

"Foote?" the proprietor said. "Little thin guy wearing a long black overcoat? Yeah, he comes in here sometimes. But I don't know where he is now."

"I'd like to find him," Harold said.

"If I was you, I'd try down near the fishing docks at the corner of Lakehurst and Viande. Foote sometimes works as a fish scaler when the pork-stuffing plant is closed."

Harold went down to the fishing docks. Here the tall ships sailed in from Cuba, Haiti, and the Bahamas. Gulls wheeled and turned in the dimming afternoon air. Small boats rolled at their moorings, their masts creaking and groaning in the stiff breeze. Many of these vessels had been decorated for Saturnalia night, now fast approaching. Tomorrow evening was the pre-Saturnalian festival. There would be a procession of boats through the harbor, lights blazing, fireworks soaring.

Harold found a ragged old man sitting on a bollard looking out to sea.

"Foote?" said the ragged old man. "Horton Foote? If you know the tracks of the morning mist you know where his pickets are."

159

"What?" said Harold.

"Kipling," the man said. "Is it really important for you to find Foote?"

"Yes, it is."

"Is it twenty bucks' worth of important?"

Harold paid. The ragged old man led him through the darkening back streets of Esmeralda, into the labyrinthine twists and turns of the inner city. It was a place where slops reeked in the gutters and sterile starlings fought rabid rats over savory bits of unkempt refuse. From somewhere on a high balcony a woman was singing a plaintive folk song, old when the pyramids were new, about the sadness of having to do the daily wash when her man warn't coming home no mo'.

Townspeople, some broad-faced and unshaven, others narrow-browed and lascivious, lounged in doorways with their hands in their pockets and clay pipes in their mouths like men waiting for Holbein to come paint their portraits. The gaslights had come on, each lamp surrounded by the glowing nimbus of light that the architects of Esmeralda had copied from an old Laird Cregar movie. Evensong was over and blue twilight was fading at last into the murmurous and irreparable night.

"That's him right over there," said the man, and sidled off into an alley.

Harold looked in the direction indicated. Across the street, at a café whose bright lights and mirrored interior made it look more important than it was, a man in a long black raincoat sat at a sidewalk table sipping a drink which, on close inspection, turned out to be a lime rickey. Sitting beside him was none other than Michelangelo Albani drinking a Negroni.

"Ah there, Harold," Albani said. "Take a seat, join us. I've just gotten here. Horton, this is my friend

Harold Erdman. He is also not interested in buying your Treachery Card."

Albani gave Harold a look that said, clear as day, "Go along with it."

"That's right," Harold said, pulling up a chair and sitting down. "I'm also not interested in buying your Treachery Card." He turned to Albani. "So what's new?"

"I got a Reckless Driving Obligation this afternoon," Albani said. "Can you imagine? And on a Bribeless Tuesday, too, of all the lousy luck. Well, you win some, you lose some. What did you do today?"

"Hey, come on, fellows," Foote said. "You think I ain't got no sources of information? I happen to know you *want* to buy my Treachery Card."

"Oh, you've seen through me," Albani said. "Yes, all right, Foote. I do want to buy it. Not *now*, of course. In a couple of weeks, a month at the most. I expect to be able to make you a very attractive offer at that time."

"I can't wait no couple of weeks," Foote said.

"So I hear," Albani said pleasantly.

"But I suspect you can't wait neither," Foote said.

Harold cleared his throat—a dead giveaway, but he didn't have Albani's experience in not giving himself away. Foote, a small, ugly man with a brownish-red birthmark shaped like a flying fish under his left armpit, rubbed his nose.

"How much do you want for it?" Albani asked.

"Two hundred dollars," Foote said.

"Done," Harold said.

Albani gave him a reproachful look, but Harold already had his billfold out.

When they were a block away, Albani said, "I could have gotten it for fifty."

"Yeah, but it's getting late."

Albani looked at his watch. Then he noticed that daytime was definitely turning into nighttime. "Damnation! We'll have to hurry if we're going to get out to Louvaine's villa tonight! And we haven't even picked out our disguises yet!"

41 • • • • •

Jacinth brought her smart little red sports car to a screeching stop in front of Louvaine's apartment building just as twilight was settling down for a short but pleasant visit to the island. The mildness of the evening was not reflected in the young girl's eyes. They were slate-blue and filled with anger.

She slammed out of her car and strode as purposefully as she could in her miniskirt and tight bolero jacket to the entrance. She didn't bother to buzz. Inserting her own key, which Louvaine had given her during a more promising time in their relationship, she went through into Louvaine's apartment.

"Louvaine?" she called. There was no answer from the darkened apartment. She turned on the lights and went to Louvaine's wardrobe closet. His chamois jacket and tweed hat were missing, and so was his shooting stick. So he *had* gone to his villa in the country, just as her friends had said, without even telling her, much less asking her. The fact that he might be on Hunt business was no excuse. She knew at least ten people he had asked to his country house for a party that night. And he hadn't asked her.

Although she was absolutely furious, she did stop to think about it, to wonder why Louvaine had decided to have this party so suddenly, and why, all personal reasons aside, he hadn't asked her.

She sat down in one of the overstuffed chairs and

lighted a mild narcotic cigarette. She remembered how Louvaine had talked about Harold. A perfect Victim type, he had called him.

And then, lo and behold, what happens but the Hunt computer, with its thousands of combinations to choose from, comes up with the very one he wanted. Something fishy there. And why had he gone out to his villa with a bunch of his friends, but not her?

All right, she said, let's reason it out. Louvaine went to the villa to party with his friends in order to lure Harold out there after him. But Harold, with this guy Albani Spotting for him, couldn't be such a fool as to do that. He wouldn't go out to a part of the island where Louvaine was well known, and, because of his habit of paying everybody off, well liked among the peasantry.

Something about this didn't make sense. It was as if one important piece of the puzzle was missing. There was some bit of information she needed, but she didn't know what it was. She got up and paced restlessly up and down the room. Her gaze fell upon the wall of framed trophies and souvenirs which Louvaine kept. She walked over to the wall, looked more closely. Yes, one of the frames was empty, a small frame with a chased silver frame. Now what had been in it? She couldn't remember. She was about to put the whole thing out of mind when, on a hunch, she turned over the frame. On the backing, in Louvaine's neat, backsloping handwriting, were the words: "This Treachery Card inherited from Uncle Osvald, may he R.I.P."

Louvaine had taken his Treachery Card! That was interesting. But who could he use it on, out at his villa where everybody was on his side? Now the mystery was only getting deeper and she needed a drink.

She went to the liquor cabinet. Near it was a telephone table, and a scratchpad was lying beside the telephone. There was a name and number scrawled on it. Horton Foote. One of Louvaine's enemies.

Again, the thing made no sense. Why would Louvaine call a man who everybody knew despised him?

She took another drag on her cigarette and sat down again. The answer came to her: Louvaine, with his devious mind, would call such a man because Foote would be the last person anyone would suspect of working for him!

What might have happened, Louvaine might have made up with Foote and paid him plenty to sell Louvaine's Treachery Card to Harold, so that Harold would think he had an advantage going out to the villa tonight, whereas actually, Louvaine would be waiting for him, ready to kill.

She didn't like it. She thought it was pretty rotten, what Louvaine had done: picked Harold out as someone he could handily kill, arranged somehow to get paired with him in a Hunt, and then set him up to fall into an ambush through a Treachery Card. Trickery was all very well, but this sort of thing was not in the Huntworld spirit.

Louvaine had left her out of the party because he had been afraid she would figure out what he was up to.

Opening the top drawer of the telephone table, she found Louvaine's telephone book. There was Harold's name, neatly written in. Louvaine couldn't have known so quickly who his Hunter was, not by any fair means!

She lifted the telephone and called the number for Harold given in Louvaine's book. It was the number of Nora's apartment. Nora answered.

"Look," Jacinth said, "you hardly know me. I'm

Jacinth Jones and we met briefly at the Jubilee Ball. You're a friend of Harold's, aren't you?"

"Yes, of course," Nora said. "What's the matter?"

Jacinth explained briefly what she had discovered. "I'm an old friend of Louvaine's, but really, he's not playing fair. He's cheating, and that's not right. So I thought I'd tell you so you could tell Harold, because I really think he ought to watch out for himself."

"Oh God," Nora said. "I just hope there's still time to stop him from going out there. He was supposed to leave from Albani's apartment. I'll call there right now. Thanks, Jacinth!"

Nora, in a blue dressing gown, her short blond hair still wet from the shower, found Albani's number and telephoned.

Teresa answered. "Albani residence."

"I must speak to Mr. Albani, or to Harold."

"They're downstairs in the basement, discussing important matters. I have orders not to disturb them for any reason whatsoever. Who is this?"

"I'm Nora Albright. I'm the person Harold has been staying with. The one from his hometown."

"Oh, yes, he's spoken of you. Would you like to leave a message? I'll have him call you as soon as he's out of conference."

"Look, this is really terribly urgent," Nora said. "I've just learned that there's been some hocus-pocus over a Treachery Card. My information is that some person named Horton Foote sold it to Albani. But I've just found out Foote is employed by Louvaine! It's a setup! If they go to the villa, Harold will be walking into an ambush!"

"Oh, mother of God, no!" Teresa said. "Mike couldn't stand it if he lost another client."

"Then you'd better call them up from the basement and let me speak to Albani or Harold."

"I'm real sorry," Teresa said, "but they're not here at all. I lied to you before."

"Why?"

"Because Mike told me to. So people would think he and Harold were still in the city."

"Then they've gone to the villa?"

"They left half an hour ago. Isn't there anything we can do? Can we inform the authorities and get them to stop the fight?"

"No," Nora said. "What Louvaine has done is not against the laws. It just runs contrary to all decency and ethics. Let me think. . . . Look, I'd better get off the phone. I've got an idea."

Nora hung up. There was no way she could contact Harold or Albani. There was no way she could get to Louvaine's villa in time. There was just one thing she could do. She hoped it would do the trick. She dialed *The Huntworld Show.*

42 • • • • •

Albani didn't like to go anywhere without his car. Man has only a limited time on earth to drive a Lamborghini and Albani wanted to take advantage of every moment of it. His professional discrimination took precedence over his personal tastes, however. With the Treachery Card in his possession he had hastily selected disguises for Harold and himself. They then went down to Central Station, arriving just in time to catch the seven-fifteen train to Santa Marta, the little village near which Louvaine had his villa.

The train was full of peasants dressed in black and carrying large woven baskets filled with salamis and breadfruits, two specialties of the island.

When Huntworld gained its independence, the Founders' first move was to kick everybody off the island in order to make a fresh start, demographically speaking. After lengthy discussions it was decided that the island needed a peasantry. But not just *any* peasantry. What Esmeralda needed was a really *good* peasantry, content with its lot and unenvious of the wealth and flashy life-styles on all sides of them. The Founders knew that a really good peasantry wouldn't be cheap, but nothing else would lend that air of quaint subservience so valued in the modern world.

After much soul-searching it was decided to import southern European peasants wearing berets. Spanish and Italian employment agencies were contacted, notices went up throughout Andalucia and the Mezzogiorno, applicants were screened, and the best applicants were sent to the well-known Peasant School in Zug, Switzerland, for final polishing.

The peasants of Esmeralda did very little real work. Their main function was decorative. Government slaves took care of the tedious tasks such as plowing, weeding, seeding, harvesting and manuring. All the Esmeraldan peasants did was perform country dances on Sundays and spend a lot of time drinking Slog, the mixture of wine and beer that the Esmeralda bottlers were trying in vain to popularize.

They also spent a lot of time boasting about how rich and virile they were while their womenfolk stayed home roasting entire pigs stuffed with ears of corn.

Their traditional costumes had been designed by Jiki of Hollywood and featured full skirts, baggy pants, and tightly laced bodices.

The children of the peasants were a problem, of course, as children always are, but soon after puberty they were sent to trade schools in Kashmir, and this made everyone happy.

An observant man might have noticed two cloaked figures getting off the train at Santa Marta del Campo, a village in the Esmeraldan countryside about fifty miles from the city. They went directly to the Blue Bophor, the largest tavern in the village, and spoke quiet words to the owner. One of the strangers, a tall, handsome man with a full false beard, showed the bartender something he held tightly in his hand. The bartender gaped at it. Then a cunning look came over his face.

"Oh, aye, and wha's thot to me?" he asked. He had attended a year of peasant bartender school in the north of England, and this showed in his speech.

"We want to see Antonio Feria," the bearded one said.

"Och, but he's busy, catering the party on the hill, you know."

"Indeed I do know." A crisp banknote appeared between his fingers. "Bring him to me, eh, there's a good fellow."

The bartender took the bill, cringed to show his gratitude, and went to the telephone.

43 •••••

When young Django Feria got home from school that evening, he found two strange men sitting in his mother's parlor. One of the men was tall and handsome and wore a false beard. The other man was even bigger, dark-haired, dressed entirely in black, and he was wearing short soft boots. There was something cold and unforgiving about his eyes—pale northern blue eyes—that struck Django at once, and he said, "Who's he?"

"Shut up," said Django's father, Antonio Feria. Django noticed that his father had put on the clean shirt with tassels which he usually saved for wakes and holidays. This stranger must be one of the important ones, Django thought, but he did not allow himself to perceive what he thought that importance might be, because the habit of not thinking what other people didn't want him to think was a lesson he had learned well in the local Peasants' Grade School.

Just then his elder sister, Miranda, came through the earthenware door. She posed for a moment, hipshot, her sultry lower lip stuck out, her hair a dense bush of untamed possibilities. She was tall for a peasant, though short for an aristocrat. Her small uptilted breasts pressed against the sleazy fabric of her peasant blouse. Her legs, completely concealed beneath her heavy long skirt, could be counted upon to be shapely.

"Father, what have you done? Who are these people?" Though her tone of voice was one of alarm, there was that in her expression which argued that she might not find it objectionable to be put into the power of one of these men, or possibly both, though perhaps not at the same time.

Antonio Feria sat down at the plain wooden table, rubbed his large unshaven jaw, and poured himself a glass of ouzette. His eyes were filled with rage struggling against lassitude.

"It's simple enough," he said gruffly. "This man"—he indicated Harold with a half-gesture of his crippled right hand—"will accompany you to Señor Louvaine's feast tonight. He will carry the teriyaki chicken in place of Giovio, the new peasant in the village whom Señor Louvaine has not met. You will accompany this man, carrying the traditional lard cupcakes. Do you understand?"

"He's not from around here," Miranda said, eyeing Harold with interest. "Is he another new peasant?"

"No, he is a Hunter, and he comes from far away."

"A Hunter? But who does he Hunt?"

Her father looked away. An expression of pain crossed his broad features. "He hunts Louvaine, El Patron," he muttered at last, pouring himself another glass of ouzette.

"Father! You would betray Señor Louvaine, who has done so much for us and for the enitre village?"

Antonio Feria grunted something unintelligible and shuffled his feet on the hard-packed dirt floor. He had several feet with him, pig's feet bought cheap from the Santa Catalina market. They were worn and bedraggled from much shuffling in the courtyard dirt.

"What choice do I have?" he demanded passionately. "The fact is, he's got the Treachery Card. You know the penalty for failure to obey a reasonable request for treachery when backed up with the Card."

"Well then," Miranda said, "it seems we have no choice. But how will we get him past the guards?"

"It will be all right—we have given him Giovio's identity card."

"But Father, Giovio is no more than five feet tall."

"So this one will have to stoop. And you will have to waggle your hips at the guards, a thing you know well how to do, as many of the neighbors have told me. You must also teach him how to shuffle."

Miranda turned to Harold. "Come with me, then. We will see what can be done."

"In a moment," Harold said. He turned to Albani. "Well, here I go."

"Do you remember the layout of the villa? We didn't have much time to study the blueprint on the train, what with that mixup over the sandwiches and then that ridiculous snake charmer."

"Yes, I've got it," Harold said. "Do you really think this will work?"

"Of course it will work. He won't suspect a thing until you drill him. Do you remember how to activate the chameleon suit? Have you got your gun? Is it loaded?"

"Yes, yes," Harold said. "Where will you be?"

"I'm going back to the tavern," Albani said. "I will drink black coffee and chew my fingernails until you come to tell me you've done it."

"Or until somebody else comes and tells you I haven't done it."

"Don't talk like that, it brings bad luck. Good luck, Harold. As we say in show business, break a leg."

Miranda came up and took Harold's arm. "Come," she said in her harsh, oddly feminine voice.

44 • • • • •

"No," Miranda said, "your back must bend more, your shoulders must hunch up, and your feet must make sliding noises as they slide over the floor."

Miranda had taken Harold to her bedroom, a small hut exactly twenty yards from her father's house—the distance prescribed by custom for marriageable peasant girls with no strong religious leanings. Here she was trying to teach him the Peasant Shuffle. He could not hope to master it all in a night, of course; at the Peasants' School in Zug they had spent an entire semester on Cringing alone. Thank God Harold would not have to learn the finer points by which exact degrees of social status are indicated, since it was unlikely that he would meet anybody. And since it was night, his postural slopitude would probably go unremarked by the drunken bodyguards in their double-breasted pinstripe suits who lounged around the outside of the villa smirking and smoking cigarettes and passing remarks to women.

"Is this any better?" Harold asked, bending over and hunching his shoulders.

"You look like a football player about to make a tackle."

"How's this? Better?"

"Now you look like a gutshot bear ready to kill anyone who comes within his reach."

Harold straightened up and stretched. "Puts a kink in your back, this Cringing."

Miranda nodded, admiring, despite her previous

resolve not to, Harold's large, solid, manly presence. Capriesti dil dnu! she thought, the ancient peasant oath coming easily to this well-studied girl. He was an attractive one. She looked at him a moment longer than necessary, then turned away. A moment later she was not surprised to find him standing very close to her, the great muzzy male presence of him so near that the smell of sweaty masculinity, combining with the fragrance of jasmine and bougainvillea borne on the dark, slow-moving night air of the dreaming tropical island, was more than merely discomfiting.

"How soon do we go to this banquet?" Harold asked her after a heart-stopping pause.

She appraised him frankly, the crackling electric depths of her dark eyes flashing a challenge that was as unanswerable as it was indecipherable, a signal as ancient and ambiguous as life itself.

"If we show up in an hour that's plenty of time," she said, her lips forming the words with a precision that argued a hidden languor.

"Then we might as well make ourselves comfortable," Harold said, lying down on the bed.

Miranda hesitated but a moment. It was perhaps her own acknowledgment that she was bidding farewell to virginity—a moment of importance for a woman each time it occurs. Damn him and his seductive clumsiness! she thought. Then she fought no longer the overriding impulse that was perhaps as close as she could come to the inner truth of things and sank down beside him on the bed with that weakness which was her hidden strength. "You sweet-talking bastard," she said, her lips sliding down the long hard straight pointer of his nose to the desired target of his mouth.

45 • • • • •

In a world without taboos against sex, drunkenness, narcotics, or murder, it is difficult to find something to do at a party that you don't do all the time anyhow. Novelty was the eternal problem of ambitious party-givers on Esmeralda.

In ancient Rome, your typical wealthy party-giver, as deficient in prudery as his present-day Huntworld counterpart, might serve the guests such rare and indigestible fare as peacock tongues stuffed with truffles and served on a bed of chilled chopped slave fat, as has been actually recorded in a papyrus found at Herculaneum.

The modish Roman dinner guest was expected to stuff this stuff down enthusiastically and then rush to the vomitorium to chuck it all up, wipe his mouth, take a pee, and get ready for the next course.

But of course in many ways your ancient Roman could not be considered truly sophisticated.

The search to find something shocking to do at a party was always a problem for Louvaine, whose desire to outrage the bourgeoisie would not have been out of place among the Dadaists.

Since nothing was forbidden in Esmeralda, the modalities of astonishment had to be reversed, the law of paradox invoked, and titillation turned into an intellectual exercise. This was the spirit in which Louvaine created the now-famous reverse strip tease.

This perverse pleasure was performed in the large dining room, immediately after the coffee and sherbets. Louvaine's guests were seated at tables arranged in a horseshoe, or, more prosaically, a U. Around the outside the servants circulated, bringing plates of food, replenishing wineglasses, serving out lines of cocaine (still popular despite the fact that the drug's potency—though not its price—had mysteriously vanished shortly after it was made legal in the United States).

The servants were all peasants from the local village, dressed now in their holiday dirndls and lederhosen. Among them a hypothetical observer might have noticed one rather larger than the others, whose clumsiness was outstanding even for a peasant. This peasant, or whatever he was, had a large bulge under his Tyrolean jacket; but perhaps it was only a bottle of wine he had squirreled away for the delectation of his boorish buddies later in the village tavern. Or it might have been something more sinister: a monstrously swollen tumor, for example, of the sort peasants in outlying areas are always displaying to visiting cameramen. It might even have been a Smith & Wesson in a shoulder holster.

At this moment all eyes were drawn to a naked young lady who entered the room and got up on the little stage set in the middle of the horseshoe or U of tables. She carried with her a shiny Samsonite suitcase on wheels, and this drew a round of polite applause. But no one was really very interested. Many of them had seen suitcases before, even ones with wheels.

But then she undid the clasps with a lascivious touch, revealing within a full wardrobe of clothing. Then a murmur ran around the diners, because they perceived that this girl was going to *put clothes on*, and this was something few of them had ever seen performed in public before.

Slowly, tantalizing, the girl drew on bra and undies and stockings. Interest became more intense as she paused over her choice of a dress, finally drawing on a fine tawny silk creation that revealed the luscious curves she had just concealed. The audience murmured in mounting excitement, whether real or feigned it was impossible to tell.

Everyone knew that, theoretically, it was possible to reverse the sweet mounting curve of the erotic and to achieve excitement through the intellectual magic of concealment. The trick in this, as in so much else, was simply in getting yourself to feel what you knew was appropriate.

Even the most insensitive got into the spirit when it came time for the reverse-strip-tease artist, now fully and daringly clothed in an outfit that included shoulder-length white gloves, to put on her fur coat. The guests could tell that something aesthetic and intellectual was going on and they were determined to wring it of its full value, whatever it was.

There was tumultuous applause when the girl finally drew a blue Russian sable around her shoulders, bowed, and left the stage. Louvaine had done it again.

The party ended soon after that. People wanted to get home early because tomorrow was a big day. It was the day of the fights in the Coliseum, the Trafficants, the Suicide Clowns, and the Big Payoff, the conclusion of which would mark the start of the Saturnalia.

Gaily the guests drove off in their supercharged limousines. A little later, the servants left in their underpowered Fiats. Louvaine had already retired to his bedroom, preparing for an early start back to the city in the morning. The guard systems went on automatically, the house lights faded, and it was night.

46 • • • • •

Night lay all around Louvaine's villa, dark and mysterious, all-pervading, implacable, suave in its sightless insinuations. The landscape, dimly illuminated by starshine and by a thin sliver of new moon, revealed shaded clumps of trees against a gray background.

Still darker was the interior of Louvaine's villa. Inside, in the scullery adjoining the kitchen, a shadow stirred among other shadows. A vagrant streak of lightning, unusual at this time of year, revealed, through the heavily meshed window, a number of potato sacks piled in a corner. One of them was moving.

Harold stood up and took off the potato sack. He had previously discarded his peasant waiter's uniform and was now clad in the chameleon suit which Albani had managed to find at the last moment in his size.

The chameleon suit, also sometimes called the ninja suit, or traje de invisibilidad, was a considerable improvement over the green-and-brown camouflage suits of earlier times, which were really effective only if you happened to be standing in a deciduous forest at dusk. The chameleon suit provided concealment for all backgrounds and decors.

Basically it consisted of a glass-fiber television screen cut and shaped by technician-tailors into a tight-fitting jumpsuit with hood and mask. The photon-mimetic material of which it was composed, through the miracle of fiber optics and laser tailoring, was capable of taking on the hues and colors of whatever background happened to be behind it.

The chameleon suit was most effective at night, of course, since black is an easy match. Against bright backgrounds, the color matching was sometimes off by five or ten spectrum-lines. Sometimes there were unexplained flashes of cold blue light, which could be embarrassing if you were trying to cross a plain background.

Fine adjustments for color had been built into the suit, of course. The one Harold wore was a new model with automatic switching for matte or gloss.

Harold moved quietly through the darkened living room, his suit taking on the patterns of the light and shadows, creating an effect like a ripple crossing the room. His gun, the faithful Smith & Wesson, was in his hand.

He heard a low growl and stopped. Looking across the room through his infrared detecting goggles, he saw the unmistakable image of a Doberman pinscher. By the angry curve in its spine Harold suspected that this was one of the famous KillKrazy strain, feared by everyone including their owners.

No one had told Harold about the Doberman. He didn't want to shoot another dog. And, too, there was the fact that it was difficult to shoot accurately in the dark even with infrared goggles.

The Doberman came over and sniffed him. Then it made a small sound in its throat like an author trying to collect his thoughts and lay down at Harold's feet.

Harold learned only later that it was Antonio Feria's dog, not Louvaine's, and that Feria had given the dog the do-not-kill-intruder-tonight command, but in his surly way had neglected to tell Harold this. A typical pointless peasant joke.

Feria hadn't deactivated his dog out of love for Harold, but because it was the law. A Huntworld high court had recently ruled that the treachery of a human may not be subverted by the loyalty of an animal which he owns but leases to someone else.

Harold went past the recumbent beast and crossed the living room. With the aid of his infrared glasses he was able to skirt the potentially noisy bric-a-brac set precariously upon rickety tables. He tiptoed around Louvaine's roller skates, left carelessly on the floor. Needle points of light from pinhead spots set in the ceiling caught glittering winks of blue from the pistol in his hand. The air was warm and faintly scented with roast beef, Yorkshire pudding, and Havana cigars: the smells of a good party. Ahead of him was the doorway to Louvaine's bedroom.

Harold took out the special magnetic pass card that Albani had acquired for him and slid it ever so gently into the slot in Louvaine's doorknob. There was a barely perceptible sound, something between a snick and a snack. Harold muttered to himself the ancient prayer of the Hunters, "Here goes nothing," and slid into the room.

Through his goggles he could make out the bed on one side of the room. A dark mound within it. He leveled the pistol. His finger tightened on the trigger. And then the lights came on.

47 • • • • •

Now Harold could see that the dark mound in the bed was Louvaine's old sleeping bag stuffed with T-shirts. Louvaine himself was seated in a comfortable armchair several feet behind Harold.

"No sudden moves, pardner," Louvaine said. "I've got you covered with my replica Model 1100 semiautomatic 20-gauge Remington shotgun. I'm loaded with 1-ounce loads of Number 8 shot backed by 11.5 grains of Red Dot powder and I'm using full-choke barrels."

"Why are you telling me all this?" Harold asked.

"Because I want you to realize that one bad move and I'll blow you all over the walls."

"They're your walls," Harold said.

"I'll have them repainted." But you could tell he didn't like the idea.

"I suppose you want me to drop the gun?" Harold asked.

"No, not at all. It'll look better if I kill you with a gun in your hand. In fact, if you try to let go of that gun I'll let you have it."

"What will you do if I don't drop the gun?"

"I'm still going to kill you," Louvaine said. "I mean, that's the whole point of the operation, isn't it? But first I'm going to gloat."

Harold thought that over in his methodical way. "Well," he said at last, "I guess you got the right."

"But I can't gloat properly unless I can see your

face. Turn slowly, and keep your gun pointed at the floor."

Harold turned as directed. Louvaine was wearing a white silk dressing gown embroidered with entwined Chinese dragons. He looked comfortable and at peace with himself, as a man might, sitting in his own bedroom with a shotgun trained on an intruder's midriff.

"I planned it all," Louvaine said. "Souzer helped me, but only with the details. It was entirely my conception—getting Foote to sell my own personal Treachery Card to that stupid Albani, luring you out here, putting the alarm systems on mock alert so you could get through to my bedroom. The fact is, you never stood a chance against me. That's because I'm smart. I'm very smart. Admit it, Harold, you're in a position to know. Aren't I smart?"

"Yes, you're smart," Harold said. He was never one to begrudge giving praise when it was due. "Congratulations, Louvaine."

"Thank you," Louvaine said.

There was a short uncomfortable silence. Then Louvaine said, "It's difficult, you know."

"What is?"

"Killing you this way. With you just standing there. Couldn't you do something provocative?"

"That's asking a little too much," Harold said.

"Yes, I suppose it is. Look, would you mind turning off that damned chameleon suit? It's getting the light values all wrong and hurting my eyes."

Harold turned off the chameleon suit and unzipped its front. The thing was really very constricting, and optical fibers don't absorb sweat worth a damn.

"Well," Louvaine said, "I guess it's getting toward that time. Too bad. I've become fond of you, Harold, in a remote sort of way." He lifted the shotgun. Harold stared at him.

"Please don't stare at me that way," Louvaine said.

Harold closed his eyes.

"No, that's no good, either."

Harold opened his eyes again.

"The fact is, I've never had to kill anybody this way. I mean, in all my other kills there's always been a lot of running around. You know what I mean?"

"I can imagine," Harold said.

"This really won't do," Louvaine said. "Look, suppose you open that window there and make a run for it."

"What will you do?"

"Wait a second or two, then blow you apart with the shotgun."

"That's what I thought," Harold said. It occurred to him that he could probably get off one shot before Louvaine fired the shotgun. With a little luck he could achieve a draw—both of them dead.

He crossed the room and sat down on Louvaine's bed. He was calculating that Louvaine might be reluctant to kill him there and have to change the sheets himself, the servants having gone home for the night.

"Well," Louvaine said, "one last gloat and then I really must finish you off even if it means sleeping tonight in the guest bedroom."

So that last remote chance was gone! Harold tensed, waiting for a moment's inattention on Louvaine's part to give him time to bring up his gun and get off a shot.

And then the room was flooded with dazzling light and thunderous noise. Startled, Harold threw himself backward over the bed and down the other side. Louvaine fired, aiming high, as usual, and taking out the ceiling lights. Downstairs the Doberman was barking hysterically. The air stank of roast beef and cordite.

The next thing Harold heard was a heavily over-amplified voice speaking through a bullhorn.

"You men in there!" the voice from the bullhorn said. "This is an official announcement! Stop firing at once! This duel is hereby suspended."

"What's going on?" Harold asked Louvaine.

"I haven't the slightest idea," Louvaine said. "They *never* stop a duel in progress . . . unless . . ."

"Unless what?"

The bedroom door opened. Gordon Philakis, m.c. of *The Huntworld Show*, came in, followed by lighting men and soundmen and a camera crew.

"Hello there, folks," Philakis said. "Here we are in the home of Louvaine Daubray, inventor of the reverse strip tease and a Hunter of great determination but little luck, at least until recently, eh, Louvaine? And the gentleman with him is Harold Erdman, a young Hunter out after his first kill, whom you may remember from yesterday's interview. How are you doing, Harold?"

"A little better now that you're here," Harold said. "But why *are* you here?"

"Your friend Miss Nora Albright phoned in and recommended your spot for the highest of honors. When we heard some of the details"—he glanced meaningfully at Louvaine—"we decided to suspend our usual random selection. Therefore, gentlemen, fight no more—until tomorrow, when you will appear in the Coliseum for the Big Payoff!"

Albani was pushing through the crowd. He put his arm around Harold's shoulders and hugged him. "Worked out just like I thought it would," he said.

"You mean *you* planned all this?" Harold asked.

"Let's just say that I anticipated the flow of events,

as a good Spotter should. The big thing is, you've made it! The Big Payoff! A ten-thousand-dollar bonus! Plus five grand for the Spotter!"

"And that's not all," said Louvaine. He walked over and put his hand on Harold's arm. His voice was husky with emotion.

"You're new here, Harold—I don't think you know what the big Payoff means. It's the highest honor a Hunter can aspire to: a chance to kill under the eyes of thousands, a chance to achieve immortality in the videotapes. It means fame, Harold, and that's what I've wanted all my life. Thank you. See you tomorrow."

He hit Harold affectionately on the arm and then walked over to where Gordon Philakis was interviewing Antonio Feria, who claimed to have set up the whole thing himself.

"Come on, let's get out of here," Albani said.

"Where are we going?"

"To get some dinner and a good night's sleep. You're in show business, Harold, and tomorrow's opening day."

48 • • • • •

The morning of the day of the Big Payoff arose serene and bright, not a cloud in the sky, a perfect day for murder. The crowds began arriving early at the Coliseum. Marching bands performed on the arena floor, each of them carrying the banner of its canton.

Below the arena, accessible by trapdoors as well as by passages from outside the amphitheater, was an entire underworld of workshops, pits for the vehicles, changing rooms for the fighters and other artists, property rooms where the weapons were stored. The repair crews were here, for both men and machines, and the men in black who would take the fallen Esmeraldan warriors to their final resting place on Boot Hill.

By midday the stands were full. They were divided into sun and shade sections as in the Spanish bullfights. The box sections were sheltered by striped awnings on poles.

It was a fine day, with the sun hot and high overhead and the girls dressed in their bright cotton finery. There was a smell in the air of meat frying in hot oil with a little garlic to keep it company. Vendors moved up and down the isles selling hot dogs, burritos, souvlaki, carnitas, drinks, drugs, programs, and T-shirts with pictures of the participants stenciled on the backs.

Children ran up and down the aisles screaming with laughter. Dogs barked. It was the sort of atmosphere of good humor which so often accompanies a total absence of good taste.

On one side of the arena there was a glass-walled control booth cantilevered out over the killing field. Television cameras were set up at strategic locations to film both the action on the field and the facial expressions of the commentators. Gordon Philakis, Mr. Huntworld himself, was at the microphone wearing a Kelly-green sports jacket with the crest of the Hunt Academy above the right breast.

"Hi, folks, this is Gorden Philakis. What a day for mayhem! Right, sports fans? We've got a sellout crowd as usual for this sporting event in the Esmeraldan year. We'll be bringing you all the action as it takes place, with slow-motion close-ups of the nasty parts. But first I'd like you to meet an old friend of ours, Colonel Rich Farrington, a man who knows a thing or two about killing."

"Thanks, Gorden, it's good to be here." Farrington was a tall, thin, gray-haired man, ramrod-straight, with a hawk nose and a thin, bloodless mouth.

"You were head of the International Mercenaries Brigade, the most colorful band of killers in the history of the world, isn't that right, Rich?"

"I sure was, Gordon, and they were wonderful days. Not all of the last war was nuclear, you know. Despite its brevity and impersonality, there *was* time for several first-class battles involving people."

"You and your boys were in the Little Chaco Campaign, weren't you, Rich?"

"We sure were, Gordon, and I can tell you that South America is still an interesting place even if the jungles *are* gone. And my boys also covered the retreat across the Limpopo. That's a river in Africa, Gordon. They were both truly spectacular fights.

The machine-gun and mortar effects alone were worth the price of admission, so to speak."

"I've watched film clips of those battles many times, Colonel, as have our viewers. The Limpopo campaign is a great family favorite. In fact, starting next season, *The Huntworld Show* is going to begin an hour-by-hour account of the entire war. You won't want to miss that one, folks. It'll be called *The Wonderful World of Bloodshed.*"

"It was a good war," Farrington said. "But I must tell you, you people right here in Huntworld in your own quiet way turn out some of the finest individual scenes of violence I've ever been privileged to witness. I'm no art critic, but I'd say that some of the stuff I've seen here has a definite surrealistic element. I'm no highbrow, God knows, but it seems to me that you people in Huntworld follow a more truly artistic vocation and turn out more products of genuine delight for more people everywhere than all these so-called artists in Europe and America mucking up canvas with meaningless colors or spoiling paper with incomprehensible words. Excuse me, Gordon, I guess I'm getting a little carried away."

"Hey, Colonel Rich, don't apologize. You're our kind of guy. A lot of *us* like stuff we can understand, too. Like killing! Nothing difficult about that! Colonel Rich, thanks for coming by."

"My pleasure, Gordon. I always come here to watch the Big Payoff and the start of the Saturnalia season. Wouldn't miss it for the world."

"Thanks again, Rich. And now I see that we're about ready to begin. Coming up will be the Suicide Clowns, who were such a heartwarming success last year, and we'll be playing the Pedestrian Game again, and Trafficulants, and the fast-moving Scythe Cycles, and finally, the Big Payoff. I hope you've all got your six-packs handy, because you don't want to miss a moment once the action starts."

49 • • • • •

Down in the stands in an expensive section of the shade, in a box sheltered by sidecurtains, Michelangelo Albani and his wife, Teresa, sat with Nora Albright. Albani was dressed in a lightweight raw-silk sports jacket the color of raw umber. He was also wearing a straw hat with black-and-white-checked ribbon, traditional for Spotters. Nora was wearing a white cotton afternoon frock, and a little red pillbox hat. Tucked up inside the hat was a black veil. She would take if down if Harold lost.

It was difficult for Nora to reconcile the Harold she had known back in Keene Valley, New York, with this Harold in Huntworld today. Here he was, a boy from her own hometown, about to take part in Huntworld's most prestigious event. And yet he was still the same old Harold, clumsy and self-confident, and very lucky.

"Are you worried?" Teresa asked.

Nora nodded. "I want him to win so badly. But I'm afraid for him. Mike, do you think he has a chance?"

"A very good chance," Albani said. "Your calling Gordon Philakis and telling him about Louvaine's treachery with the Treachery Card was brilliant. It got us this event, the Big Payoff, the top fight of the year. And now Harold's got the psychological edge, nothing's going to stop him. Try to relax and enjoy the games."

"I'll try," Nora said. She dabbled at her eye with a tiny handkerchief. "But I don't know if I can."

"The Suicide Clowns are coming up," Albani said. "You like the Suicide Clowns, don't you?"

Nora's expression brightened. "Yes, they're always fun."

"Relax and enjoy. Now I must go downstairs and prepare Harold for his contest. Don't worry about him, my dear. He has luck, and that's more valuable than skill any day."

50 • • • • •

Down on the arena floor the Suicide Clowns had just come out, to heavy applause. There were always a lot of applications from all over the world for one of the coveted yearly positions as a Suicide Clown. Some people felt that if your death made somebody happy it wasn't in vain after all.

"Today," Philakis said, "we're lucky to have with us Mr. Tommy Edwards, director and production manager of Huntworld's Suicide Clown School. He and I going to provide a commentary to the clowns' antics. Hi, Tommy."

"Hi, Gordon. Well, I see that the action is just about to begin."

"That's right, Tommy. Stagehands are out on the arena floor erecting a two-story structure. It's a replica of an old-fashioned bank. This looks like a good number coming up. What do you call this, Tommy?"

"This is called 'The Bank Robbery.' It's based on an old Keystone Cops skit."

"All right," Philakis said, "the bank is filled with customers and tellers, all in clown costumes. It looks like a normal busy day in a small-town American bank of a hundred or so years ago. Now the Keystone bank robbers drive out in two flashy open convertibles. The Keystone bank robbers are dressed in funny costumes, and they have comically painted faces. They enter the bank waving their weapons. They rob the bank. One teller tries to resist. A robber shoots him. The teller expires, blowing kisses to the audience. That's pretty cute, Tommy."

"Thanks, Gordon. Now the robbers take their loot, conveniently packaged in small canvas sacks with dollar signs stenciled on their sides, run out of the bank, and pile into their cars. From one of the arena doorways another old-fashioned convertible comes racing through. It is a police car filled with the Huntworld Keystone Cops. The bank robbers drive away in a hail of bullets. Several innocent bystanders are killed. They are also Suicide Clowns, of course."

"The cars are chasing each other around the arena," Philakis went on. "They're dodging obstacles which the stagehands set up, exchanging shots, throwing hand grenades at each other. People are getting killed in both vehicles. The robbers end up back at the bank. They run inside, barricade themselves in the upper stories. More Suicide Clown police come on. It's a siege. The police bring up heavy machine guns and mortars. Suicide Clowns are blown away right and left, sailing through the air in comical poses. The audience really loves it. We'll study the tapes later, but I can tell you right now that this is a scene of carnage I've rarely seen excelled in previous years. What do you think, Tommy?"

"I agree, Gordon. You know, it's amazing how many bullets a body can absorb and still keep on going and pulling that trigger and pouring bullets into another body. It sort of gives you a good feeling about human tenacity, doesn't it?"

"I'll say it does, Tommy."

"I'd like to remind the audience once again that this is the highest destiny that any really serious suicide can hope to attain: dying in front of the cameras on *The Huntworld Show* on the day before Saturnalia."

"We're down to just eight clowns now, Tommy. Do

you think they're getting a little—well—faint-hearted? They've been at it for quite a while, in terms of actual combat conditions."

"Oh, these boys aren't about to quit, Gordon. Not the way we train them at the Esmeralda Suicide Clown School."

"Tommy, why don't you tell the folks something about our famous school while the surviving clowns take a few moments to reload?"

"Well, Gordon, as you know, ethics have changed a great deal since suicide became legal in most civilized countries of the world. Most countries don't any longer penalize would-be suicides who fail or lose their nerve. But we in Huntworld believe that if a law's worth having, it's worth enforcing. Once a person is accepted in the Suicide Clowns, he signs a pledge to kill himself when and in the manner prescribed by the director and production manager or his assistants. You see, theatrically speaking, a suicide that doesn't happen is just a fizzle."

"Perhaps you could tell these folks how you enforce the contracts. I mean, suppose a Suicide Clown refuses to kill himself or let himself be killed as the production manager directed. What would you do? Execute him?"

"Certainly not. That would be just what he wanted: somebody else to take responsibility for his death. No, Gordon, if a Suicide Clown defaults, the penalty is very simple. He has to paint his nose red and wear a sign on his back which says 'Chicken.' And go on living as long as possible. It doesn't happen often, I can assure you."

"I'd think not, Tommy," Gorden Philakis said. "Now I see the surviving Clowns have finished reloading and are ready to go at it again. They're coming out from behind their barricades, guns ready but not firing. They're forming a circle. A Clown in the costume of a ringmaster has walked to the center of the circle. He has on a tall black silk hat. He takes it off. A pigeon escapes from beneath. It is the signal.

"Everybody blazes away! Bodies flop and fly apart! Wow, just look at that blood! It's one hell of a finish! Listen to the applause!

"And look! The ringmaster has somehow survived, even though he was at the center of it all. He's badly wounded, struggling to his feet. He's still holding on to his silk hat. He manages to stand up. He salutes the audience and puts on the hat . . .

"And the top of his head blows off! A bomb inside the hat! First the bird and then the bomb! What a good finish! Oh, yes, Tommy, that was a *really* good finish. How did you ever think up that one?"

"Thinking it up wasn't so difficult, Gordon. It was rehearsing it that posed the problems."

51 •••••

Down in the artists' section below the arena, in a private dressing room with a star over the door, Albani was giving Harold a back rub and some good last-minute advice.

"I don't know what form this duel is going to take. They pull something new every year. The Elders of the Hunt Academy make their decision at the last minute. So remember what Chang told you. Expect the unexpected. You feeling OK?"

"You know," Harold said, "it really is fun. Hunting, I mean. It's just too bad someone has to get killed. I don't suppose it would work out all right without that, but it's too bad anyhow."

"You keep on with thoughts like that and you're going to have a short afternoon," Albani said.

"I'm not going to let him kill me," Harold said.

In another private dressing room in another part of the artists' section, also with a star over the door, Louvaine sat with his Spotter, Souzer. There was a third man in the dressing room: George Sachs, the special trainer Louvaine had hired for this event.

Sachs was fat and stupid and had boorish manners and bad body odor. All these defects were outweighed by a single virtue. Sachs's brother-in-law, Hostilius Vira, was chief weaponer for the Huntworld Games. That meant Vira was one of the first to know what weapons and special equipment would be needed for this year's Big Payoff. And since Vira was a family man and felt sorry for his sister, Petrilla, Sachs was able to get information from his brother-in-law regarding the type of combat to be selected.

"But where *is* the information?" Louvaine asked, the *n* vibrating unpleasantly in his nose.

"I don't know what's keeping him," Sachs said. "Vira's never been this late before. He should have telephoned me half an hour ago."

"He'd better do it soon," Louvaine said. "Otherwise this junk'll be useless." He gestured at the two large canvas sacks that he and Souzer had lugged into the arena past a bribed guard. "I'll be going on soon. These little subterfuges will be useless unless I know what I'm up against."

"Everything's gonna be okay, boss," Sachs said, his thick lips moving so obscenely that they seemed to sully the very words he uttered, rendering them unfit to ever be used again.

Just then the telephone rang.

52 • • • • •

"Joining us now," Gordon Philakis said, "is Mel Prott, a former three-time winner of the 1000-cc scythe-cycle event. Glad to have you with us tonight, Mel."

"Glad to be here, Gordon," said Prott. He was a beefy man with a head of tight blond curls. Like Philakis he was wearing a green blazer with the Huntworld insignia emblazoned over the right breast.

"I see that they have the barriers already in place for the Game of Pedestrians. For those of you new to the show, I'll just say that the structure they are erecting down there is known as the maze. It's a pretty simple maze, and the passage through it is just wide enough for a sports car. The turns are tight, but they're banked, so the drivers can take them at good speeds. Why don't you tell us some more about this event, Mel?"

"Well, it's simple enough," Prott said. "You have a pedestrian down there in the maze with the motorist. The motorist has his car, the pedestrian has his hand grenades. They go one on one in the maze. Only one man walks or drives away."

"The pedestrian has five hand grenades, isn't that right, Mel?"

"That's right, Gordon. He usually carries one in each hand and three clipped to his belt. There have been pedestrians who carried an extra grenade in their teeth, but most experts agree that slows you down."

"For those of you watching this event for the first time," Gordon Philakis said, "I should point out that the walls of the maze are pierced here and there by openings just large enough for a man to duck through. That's important when the motorist is racing down a straightaway at you."

"And we should also mention," Mel Prott said, "the grenades have a default setting of one and one half seconds. But you can decrease the time with thumb pressure to half a second."

"That's cutting it pretty fine, though, isn't it, Mel?"

"It sure is," Prott said. "You have to throw the grenade with the car just about on top of you, and then dive through the hole before the blast wipes you out along with the car. It takes a fine judgment, I can assure you."

"Car and driver are now moving through the maze," Philakis said. "The car is flashing silver in the sun. It's a Porsche, the 1600 Normal, one of the old models favored for running down pedestrians, in mazes. Pedestrian and motorist are in the maze now, firing at each other with the .22 caliber target pistols provided for a little extra excitement. The motorist is coming around a turn, the pedestrian has ducked through one of the holes, now he's come back out again, he's behind the motorist just as he has to slow for a turn. The pedestrian's arm is back, he's ready to throw the grenade. But what's this . . ."

"The motorist was ready for him," Mel Prott said. "Preparation and anticipation, that's what you need in an event like this. The motorist is in reverse now, backing up fast. The pedestrian has thrown his first grenade, but he put too much on the pitch, it explodes high in the air. Now he's scrambling to get out of the way, he's racing for a hole, he's tumbled through it. But I think he took a glancing blow from the car's onside fender."

"He's dazed, uncertain," Philakis said. "Here comes the Porsche again down the straightaway, accelerating nicely. The pedestrian is up, he's fumbling for a grenade—"

"Too late," Prott said.

The Porsche reversed again, disappearing around a corner. The pedestrian looked around desperately, trying to locate it. Suddenly there it was, coming at him from the other side. The crowd was cheering wildly.

The pedestrian was caught on a straightaway. He looked frantically for a hole, but none was close enough. Convulsively he threw a grenade at the onrushing car. The setting must have been wrong, because it bounced off the car's roof and exploded harmlessly behind the onrushing vehicle.

By the time it went off the pedestrian was as dead as last year's herring, a red mess spread-eagled over the Porsche's front grille. Men came out, carted off the wreckage, and hosed down the track, and it was time for the next pair.

53 • • • • •

"They've cleared away the maze now," Gordon Philakis said, "and here comes the vehicles for the Trafficulant event. What a glittering procession of mobile weaponry! You can go a long way before you find something a man likes more than a personal fighting vehicle. Mel, why don't you tell us something about this contest?"

"It's basically your old demolition-derby format," Prott said. "Only in the game of Trafficulants, instead of just running around a track and slamming into each other, our vehicles are armored and equipped with cannon and other kinds of weaponry. So what you get here is essentially a battle of tanks and armored cars on the popular level."

"I think we should mention," Philakis said, "that all the shells used by the contestants are supplied by the Hunt Academy Armorers and are fused to explode twenty feet from the muzzle. That's to ensure that stray rounds don't go into the crowd."

"Is that a rocket launcher on the roof of that Lincoln?" Prott asked.

"That's just what it is," Philakis said. "Autoloading, self-aiming. And I see that the Toyota Special has a cannon mounted at either end."

"Here comes the Mourlan Spider," Mel Prott said. "It's got a 2,000-horsepower engine and a claw arm operated from a crane mounted on the rear. The claw itself works through the dashboard computer."

"Here's Eddie's Ram," Philakis said, "a car shaped

like one of those old dinosaurs—a stegosaurus, I believe. The dinosaur theme has always been popular in assault-car design. It's completely armored all around and works with a periscope system. It's jockeying for position. There's the signal! The event of Trafficulants has begun!"

"Eddie's Ram hasn't wasted no time," Mel Prott said. "It's powerful magnet has gripped Maxwell's Monster. A panel in the Ram's side has opened, and out comes a carbon-tipped circular saw. It's going through the armor plating like a knife through butter. Now the telescoping robot arm has planted the explosive charge."

"Beautiful," Mel said.

"And here comes Kelly's Scorpion, built for speed and maneuverability like one of the old Formula 1 racers, low to the ground, difficult to get a grip on and hard to hit."

Down on the yellow sand of the arena the battle raged. Clouds of white smoke rose into the cloudless blue sky as the cars turned and slewed, hammering at each other with cannon at short range. Grease and blood and spare parts began to appear on the arena sands. Cars wheeled and turned, blowing off each other's tires and doors or ramming their opponents into the arena walls.

Soon there were only two fighters moving, the Scorpion and the Egg Layer.

"These two fighting vehicles have entirely different approaches," Philakis said. "Want to tell us about them, Mel?"

"The Scorpion is as close to a hummingbird as you can get on wheels. With its 360-degree four-wheel-capability steering, it can turn and dart off at unexpected angles. Its built-in randomized steering program renders it difficult for an enemy computer to get a fix. It has a heavy machine gun firing explosive rounds mounted in front. But it's real punch is in the heavy cannon mounted in the rear."

"What a contrast with the Egg Layer," Philakis said, "which is built along entirely different principles. Egg-shaped, as its name implies, and painted a matte black, its twenty-four-point steel armor adds greatly to its weight but renders it impervious to anything but a direct hit at close range. The Egg Layer presents no show of offensive weapons, no gun ports or turrets, no muzzles sticking out, not even an antenna. It defends itself by laying mines in the path of opposing vehicles."

The Scorpion darted past the Egg Layer, a flash of gold in the afternoon sun. The vehicle slewed around, and its powerful rear gun trained on the Egg Layer's flank. At that moment, the ground beneath the Scorpion erupted. The car was thrown twenty feet straight up in the air and came down in six large pieces and many smaller ones.

"Well, how about that!" Philakis said. "Looks to me like the Scorpion underestimated the Egg Layer's rapid mine-laying capability, thinking perhaps that a flank attack would be safe. The car is moving into the victory circle now. What a mess down there! But what a fine rousing finish!"

"Sure is," Mel Prott said. "I always love to see the big cars slug it out. It'll be bloody pistons in the old garage tonight."

54 • • • • •

"You're sure about that?" Louvaine said to Sachs.

"I'm sure about what my brother-in-law told me," Sachs said.

"Damnation," Louvaine said. "I didn't expect it to be that. What a weird idea. Souzer, we got anything to cover this situation?"

Souzer smiled. "I was expecting something like this. And I packed the right equipment."

He opened one of the canvas bags. "Come on, boss, let's hurry. You're on soon."

55 •••••

"Next come the scythe-cycle events," Philakis said. "Mel, why don't you tell us something about them, seeing as how you're a three-time winner of this event."

"Well sure, Gordon. As you can all see, the cyclists have long, razor-sharp scythes attached to their hub-caps, like the Romans used to have on their battle chariots. The men on foot are armed with net and trident like the ancient Roman gladiators from whom we adopted the custom. The question is, can the man on foot get the man on the bike before the man on the bike gets him? That's oversimplifying it, but that's what it basically comes down to."

"Sometimes it seems as if the cyclists are at a disadvantage," Philakas said. "After all, they have to drive and balance their vehicles no matter what else they do. When the netman throws his net, even if it misses, it's sure to divide the driver's attention, throw him off stride, give the netman time to dart in behind the flashing scythes and take down the driver with his trident."

"That's true, of course, Gordon," Mel said. "But the cyclists have developed their own strategies to deal with that situation. Their short, light, powerful bikes can make astonishing stops, turns, and slides. They can lay them down flat and come back an instant later with the rear wheel digging. They can slide their bikes rear end first into the netman, hooking him at the knees. Sometimes they can grab the net without losing control of the bike and pull the netman around the arena behind them until he's a pile of rags, if you'll excuse the expression. So it's not all in favor of the netmen."

Down in the arena the event had begun. Motorcycles snarled and screamed, some of them spinning out of control, their drivers caught in the nets, twisting and turning, trying to escape the deadly tridents. Some of the netmen were down, too, screaming as the scythes cut them apart.

Limbs and heads rolled on the bloody sand.

The crowd was weak with emotion when the last two survivors, one netman and one cyclist, were announced winners of the melee.

56 • • • • •

There was a short intermission to give everyone time to get refreshments and go to the toilet. During this time the high wire was set up for the high-wire duelists.

A hundred feet above the arena floor, the fencers came out on the high wire. Each man was clad in a one-piece suit of stretch satin. Their pointed foils winked in the sun. They advanced toward each other. Each man had a wire noose secured around his neck and leading back to a large reel. The reel allowed a man to move backward and forward on the wire without interfering with his movements. But if he should happen to fall from the high wire, he would drop no more than fifty feet before reaching the end of his wire. Then, with a sudden jerk, his neck was broken.

It was an eccentric sort of event, even for Esmeralda, and needed a special kind of person to volunteer to do it. Luckily, the human race has never thought up anything so ludicrous, dangerous, and frivolous that it won't attract many willing volunteers.

The antagonists met at the midpoint, tapped swords, and the duel was on.

In this sort of fencing, your movements must be both minimal and precise. Lunges and parries, too, required a certain lightness of touch. Sometimes it was better to take a hit than, by warding it off too vehemently, be cast from the wire.

The man on the left, Augustin Smiles, a two-times-past winner from Slot, North Dakota, advanced lightly on slippered feet, his rapier a flickering snake's tongue. His opponent, Gerard Gateau from Paris, France, was a new contestant. Nobody knew his form.

Smiles led off boldly. Gateau retreated before the North Dakotan's strong advance. The Frenchman parried violently, and then whipped a blow at Smiles saber-fashion. This was within the rules but was unheard of in practice, because of the danger of propelling oneself off the wire through the sudden explosive production of torque. This was common knowledge. But Gateau did not seem to care for the established parameters of the high-wire duel. Instead of trying to dampen the wire's wavelike oscillations, he swung his body again, increasing them.

Philakis was one of the few in the crowd knowledgeable enough to know that Gateau was one of the new high-wire theorists which Paris had recently produced. From their coffee shops on the Rue St. Denis, Gateau and others had been proclaiming to the world that oscillation was but another form of stability; but they had been proclaiming it in French, and so nobody in Great Britain or America had understood them.

Now Gateau was here to prove his assertion.

Smiles, the gaunt North Dakotan, fought to keep his balance. No use—the stability upon which he relied no longer existed. Arms flailing wildly, he fell from the wire.

A gasp went up from the crowd. Then a great cheer as Gateau, just as his opponent's fall began, skewered Smiles neatly through the heart, thus enabling him to die of a wound more noble than a broken neck.

But the move put Gateau himself into trouble. Now it was his turn to flail his arms, to feel the oscillation of the wire become more than he could control, to hang there for a heartbeat, impossibly trying to ride the wire as it swung like a giant jumprope in the hands of two peevish and enormous little girls.

Then Gateau fell. But his sangfroid did not abandon him, nor did his cool. Releasing the sword, he grasped the neck wire with both hands, bringing himself to a stop before his descent could build up an insurmountable momentum. He hung there for a moment, making small kicking movements of the feet in acknowledgment of the crowd's cheers, and then climbed up the neck wire hand over hand, back to the high wire.

After acknowledging the crowd's applause he cried, indicating the trembling wire, "You see? It *did* move!"

There was a lot of discussion in the newspapers the next day as to what he meant by that.

Next came the Death Frisbee contest. The two players advanced into the center of the arena and saluted the crowd and the referee, who was protected for this event by plate armor from head to toe. He raised his checkered flag, dropped it. The fight had begun.

The Frisbees for this event were made of light steel plate, and their edges were razor-sharp. The contestants wore no protective armor. They were clad only in bathing suits and sneakers. Their only means of defense were the heavy leather gauntlets they wore, whose inner surfaces were protected by three layers of mesh steel. Only with a glove like this could a Death Frisbee safely be caught.

The Frisbees soared, arced, and fluttered back and forth across the arena. An early use was seen of the boomerang shot, in which the Frisbee, if it missed its target, arced around and returned to its owner's glove. Both men were adept at skimming the deadly missiles along the ground, to dart upward at unexpected moments.

The shiny steel-blue Frisbees soared and winked in the sun, buzzed like enraged hornets, darted and fluttered like a flock of bats settling off into the sunset.

For a while the duel swayed back and forth inconclusively. The crowd watched in rapt silence. No sound could be heard but the metallic chunk as a Frisbee was caught in a protective glove. Each man had a sack of spare Frisbees carried in a broad leather pouch on his back.

The favorite this year was Oscar Szabo. He was facing Manuel Echeverria, Manos, as he was nicknamed, a Spanish Basque from Bilbao. Echeverria had been training in secret. No one knew what kind of moves he had.

Early in the fight it was evident that Manos's catches were not as crisp as Oscar's, and the Basque seemed a trifle unsteady on his feet, as though he had been partying too long the previous night, which was in fact the case.

The hulking Hungarian sensed his advantage and began to edge forward, pushing back his opponent with a quick succession of throws that dipped and fluttered crazily like a flight of starlings high on paraquat. Manos retreated, bobbing and weaving as the Death Frisbees swooped toward him, batting them away with his glove-clad fists, trying to keep his balance.

It seemed like the finish for the Boozy Basque. But aficionados of the sport who had seen Manos play in Europe nudged their less knowledgeable companions in the ribs and said, "Watch this!"

And sure enough, just as it seemed like the end for the Bumbling Basque, Manos suddenly made a neat double sidestep and reached into his basket, took out two Frisbees, and flung them simultaneously. Yes, the bloody old Basque was ambidextrous, and well trained in the intricacies of the two-handed Frisbee attack!

The gleaming saucers of slaughter came swooping at Szabo from different directions and angles, delivered with incredible speed and spin, arriving as near to simultaneity as makes no never-mind. In desperation the Hairless Hungarian fell on his back, kicking away the buzzing Frisbees that came at him like black flies in June with the desperate fly swatters of his steel-shod feet.

Even in this posture Szabo was able to perform the desperation bolo throw that had won the prize for him last year. His Frisbee screamed through the air, swung toward the stands, curved around, and flew toward Manos from an oblique angle.

The Basque was up to the challenge. His left-handed counterthrow collided with his opponent's Frisbee in midair, causing sparks to fly, redirecting both Frisbees harmlessly into the stands.

Then Manos spun around three times like a discus thrower and flung two Frisbees simultaneously.

The saucer-shaped missiles arced high into the air and curved in at Szabo from different directions, traveling like out-of-control locomotives.

Szabo managed to catch one; the other severed his left arm just above the elbow.

Ignoring the injury, Szabo tried to set himself for one final throw. Before he could let go, another double Frisbee salvo came fluttering at him from opposite sides.

One was a near miss. The other sliced through the Hungarian's head just above the eyebrows.

A boom mike caught his last expiring gurgle and amplified it for the cheering crowd.

And then it was time for the Big Payoff.

57 • • • • •

The last of the carnage left by the scythe cyclists had been cleared away. "And now, ladies and gentlemen," Gordon Philakis announced, "the event you have all been waiting for, at whose conclusion Saturnalia officially begins. Yes, friends, it's time for the Big Payoff! I know you've all been wondering what form it's going to take this year. So let's not waste any more time. Ok, boys, set it up."

Men in white jumpsuits came out into the arena wheeling a large raised platform enclosed with ropes, like a boxing ring only larger. A groan of disappointment arose from the audience when they saw it.

"Now wait just a minute," Philakis said to the crowd. "It's not what you think. You probably think it's going to be a simple gladiatorial event like we had last year, right? Wrong! We've got a little switch this time, and we think it'll be a lot of fun. But first let me introduce our lucky finalists. Come on out here, boys."

Harold and Louvaine came out through different gateways to thunderous applause. Both were dressed in black one-piece-suits.

Four Big Payoff attendants came out with them, carrying between them a large wooden box.

"Here they are, folks," Philakis said, "our two Big Payoff players, our local boy, Louvaine Daubray, and his opponent, a newcomer to our fair shores, Harold Erdman. Only one of them is going to come out of that ring alive, and he will be our new King of

Saturnalia. How you feeling, boys? Louvaine, how does it feel to be in the Big Payoff? I hear you've been wanting this honor for a long time."

"I can only say," Louvaine said, "that although I don't really deserve it, I'm deeply aware of the honor bestowed on me and I promise to give everyone a good fight."

"Spoken like a true Hunter!" Philakis said. "And what about you, Harold?"

"What? Oh, all that stuff he said, that's what I mean, too. But I really do mean it!"

"Good luck to both of you. And now, let's take a look at the weapons."

The attendants opened the box and removed from it two glittering daggers.

"That's for the close-in fighting," Philakis said, "but here is the main armament."

The attendants took from the box two short-handled, double-bladed battleaxes and held them up for everyone to see. The cameras zoomed in for a closer look.

"Aren't they beauties?" Philakis said. "They're exact replicas of an old Norse model. These axes were manufactured right here in our own Hunt Armory and sharpened to a degree that we suspect the old Norsemen knew nothing about. Full-size working replicas of these axes will be on sale at the exits immediately after this event. But that's later. For now, these boys are going to get into that ring and have it out. How about that, folks?"

There was a polite round of applause.

"Now, friends," Philakis said, "I've got a feeling that some of you are just a little disappointed. You're probably thinking, well, yes, battleaxes, that's nice, but it's not all that different from last year's underwater sword fight. Well, friends, the Elders of your Hunt Academy have thought long and hard and have taken steps to ensure that this fight with battleaxes will be a little different from what you might have expected. . . . Okay, boys, show them the rest of the stuff."

The attendants on the arena floor had been standing at attention around the raised platform. Now they stripped off the canvas that covered it. Beneath was a glassy surface. Sunlight bounced off it in dazzling reflections.

A murmur of appreciation came up from the crowd.

"Now," Philakis said, "you're probably asking yourself, what is that shiny stuff? Well, friends, that shiny stuff is something we don't see much of here in Esmeralda except in our drinks. That is *ice*, ladies and gentlemen, and it's kept in superhard, superslick condition by the portable refrigeration units stored underneath the platform's apron. Let's have a round of applause for TWA, which flew in this unit for us from Miami's Iceworld on short notice."

There was a round of applause.

"And now for the final piece of equipment." Philakis gestured at the attendants standing beside Harold and Louvaine with the wooden box. The attendants opened the box once more and removed from it two pairs of lace-up ice skates.

First there was a titter of amusement in the crowd, then growing applause as the idea caught on. Philakis socked it home.

"Yes, friends, men with battleaxes on ice skates! What do you think, Mel?"

"I've seen a lot of these Payoffs," Mel said, in a husky confidential voice, "but this one really looks like something special. I would predict, Gordon, that this event should prove a new high in bloodshed and merriment."

"I think so too, Mel. And now, what about a round

of applause for our researchers, who, by methods known only to themselves, learned the shoe sizes of our contestants?"

There was more applause.

"Boys, you'll find that your names have been appliquéd on the sides of your skates. Contestants, suit up!"

58 • • • • •

The afternoon was beginning to wane. The ice rink was bathed in spotlights. The referee motioned the two men to come to the center of the rink.

Harold skated out cautiously, uncertain of his balance. He had done a little skating back home, probably more than Louvaine had ever done. Given his size and weight, this sort of a contest ought to favor him.

But he suspected that Louvaine had something up his sleeve. The guy didn't look worried enough. He was even grinning at him!

And he seemed to skate pretty well, too.

The referee reminded them that there would be no rounds and no breaks, and that anything they did to each other was legal. A tie would be declared if both men were too badly wounded to proceed. In that case, the referee would flip a coin to decide who was to be the winner and who the decedent. Only one man could come out of the ring alive.

Harold skated back to the little stool provided for him. Albani rubbed the back of his neck in the immemorial gesture of all trainers.

"The thing to remember," Albani said, "is that each action has an equal and opposite reaction. That means a lot when you're swinging a battleax."

"What bothers me," Harold said, "is that Louvaine looks too sure of himself. And he seems to skate pretty well, too."

"He's just bluffing, trying to psych you out," Albani said.

In fact, he had been thinking the same thing. Thank God he'd get the Spotter's bonus whether Harold won or lost. Not that he was indifferent to the outcome, but one did have to be practical.

"It's like Louvaine knows something we don't know," Harold said.

"If I see anything fishy," Albani said, "I'll lodge an immediate protest. It'll be too late, but I'll see that your reputation is vindicated."

The bell rang.

"Whatever he's got," Albani said, "you've got better. You're going to win this, Harold. Go in there and get 'em, kid!"

Harold skated out and the fight was on.

59 • • • • •

Souzer, sitting in Louvaine's corner, watched as the skaters circled each other warily, staying just out of striking distance. Louvaine looked pretty good on those skates. That winter he'd spent in Switzerland had really paid off. Harold didn't look so bad, either. But Harold didn't have the edge.

There had been ice-skating duels before in Huntworld. Souzer had been prepared for this eventuality. He had prepared the skates himself with the help of a machinist friend.

Tiny needle-sharp points had been welded to the front part of the skating blade where it curls upward toward the toe. By standing on his toes, Louvaine would have excellent purchase. By spiking his skates firmly into the ice at the right moment, he'd be able to brace himself for the killing blow. That should give him all the advantage he needed.

That, plus the fact that he was well trained in the use of the battleax. Indeed, he had represented his country in the ax-dueling competition in the last Olympics.

With a country as small as Esmeralda, that didn't necessarily argue a high level of skill. But it was something, and presumably more than Harold had going for him. Harold had only his luck, and that had about run out.

Louvaine and Harold were skating faster now, circling, turning, sweeping around each other, a *pas de deux* of death on ice to the accompaniment of the Huntworld orchestra playing selections from Tchaikovsky's *Swan Lake*.

The battleaxes glinted steely blue under the spotlights. The fighters feinted and swung, forehand and backhand, grunting, stumbling, and revolving with the force of their efforts.

Louvaine scored a lucky glancing blow off Harold's left shoulder, drawing blood.

Harold spun around like a top, striking out blindly.

Louvaine ducked, came up again, swung the ax, went off balance, careened into the ropes, came off them, found Harold circling in toward him, ax at the ready.

Gordon Philakis's excited commentary could be heard above the thunder of the crowd. The crowd were on their feet and yelling. Even the pickpockets had forgotten business for a moment, watching the peak spectacle of the Esmeraldan year.

Souzer could tell when Louvaine was ready to make his killing move. A certain look came over his face. A second later Louvaine was moving into action. He crowded Harold toward a neutral corner, feinting with the ax. Then he went up on his toes. His battleax was poised over his right shoulder. He swung a broad downward sweep, a deadly cut impossible for a man on skates to avoid.

Harold dodged it in the only possible way. He fell down and slid across the ice.

Louvaine's arm came back again with the battleax. He ran forward on steel points and began the deadly backswing designed to carve Harold into pork chops.

Harold was a few feet away, down flat on the ice, still spinning slightly, unable to stabilize himself. He did the only thing he could do. He released the battleax, a quick wrist throw with a lot of spin on it.

The ax skittered across the ice toward Louvaine's

feet. Louvaine jumped back to avoid it. He came down flat on his skates, and they shot out from under him.

Harold managed to stop himself from spinning and scrambled to his feet and fell again. He couldn't find his ax. He was helpless. He threw his hands over his head, waiting for the killing blow.

But Louvaine was still down on the ice. He was lying in a widening pool of blood. The crowd was screaming. It took Harold a moment to realize that Louvaine had fallen on top of the ax. One head had imbedded itself in the ice. The other head had cut into Louvaine's spine.

Harold scrambled on hands and feet across the ice. He cradled Louvaine in his arms. A wave of pity came over him. "You're going to be all right!" he cried.

Louvaine coughed pathetically. "Actually, I don't think so. 'Tis not as deep as a well nor as wide as a church door, but 'twill do.' I always thought Mercutio the most appealing of Shakespeare's characters, much more interesting than that sappy Romeo."

"Oh, Louvaine," Harold said, "I'm sorry it had to be you. I've come to like you, dammit."

"And I like you, too," Louvaine said. "But we would never have become friends if we hadn't been trying to kill each other. Droll, isn't it? Goodbye, Harold. Oh, one last thing."

"Yes?" said Harold, bending to hear the faltering words.

"Tell them to bury me under my Indian name. It is Un-ko-Pi-Kas, He Who Laughs First, in the language of the Algonquins."

"How did you get an Indian name?" Harold asked.

Louvaine smiled wanly. "If only I had time to tell you!" His eyelids fluttered, then lay still on his cheeks like gased moths.

Harold threw back his head and let out a great shouting howl of grief and anger and triumph. And then the crowd had broken into the ring and carried him away on their shoulders to be crowned winner of the Big Payoff and King of Saturnalia.

About the Author

Robert Sheckley is best known for his off-beat, witty short stories, which he began writing in 1951. He was a protégé of Horace Gold, former editor of *Galaxy*, a magazine in which many of his early stories appeared, and by the mid-1960s he had already produced a significant body of work that was widely acknowledged to be at the forefront of science fiction. His bestseller, THE TENTH VICTIM, and the subsequent movie, launched his reputation far beyond genre classification. Mr. Sheckley has also had a major influence on his fellow writers as fiction editor of *Omni* magazine. At present he is at work on VICTIM/HUNTER, the third book in the series begun with THE TENTH VICTIM.